JOURNEYS

An Anthology

C'Anna Bergman-Hill

ISBN: 0997850019
ISBN 13: 9780997850017

FOR VIOLA

I can see you
at the end of the day
in the darkness
corner chair
a pool of lamp light
traveling thousands of miles
in your reading journeys

A SUGGESTION . . .

These stories are intended to deepen the reading of *Junctions*, and to be read after the novel.

the author

TABLE OF CONTENTS

IF YOU LEAVE A PLACE

If you leave a place, it will never wholly leave you.
If you loved the harmonies of the train whistle
    it will follow you where there is no train
    and weave itself into the wind whistle
    so that behind the work you're lost in
    distantly the train sings past . . .
and if you did not love that sound
    it will do the same.

If you leave a place, you can discover your other selves,
    those you invented out of novels and daydreams,
    and day by day live that complex other self into solid life.
    Someday you will hear someone tell you
    that the very essence of you
    is that new self you invented,
and the thought of the place and self you left comes to you
    like a dream, like a reproach, like a memory of a book
        you read.

Jinx McCombs

1

THE JOURNEY BEGAN IN SORROW

Pedro

1925 - 2005

Late in the summer of 1948, Pedro Sanchez stepped off a bus and walked into the town of Pine Junction, his inexpensive new saddle oxfords crunching the gravel road. He had one goal, and it was monumental: to create a new beginning for a radically different reality. He had a heavy stake in leaving the past behind, and spent the rest of his days keeping his history at bay. Through the years, he was so successful at maintaining this distance between the old and the new, that he could almost pretend existence began for him that summer day.

Despite his iron will and his work ethic, and his ability to completely immerse himself in any given academic topic, despite his beautiful new family, Pedro was never completely free of the nightmares. As a college student he had sweated them out alone. When he married Victoria, she held him through the worst of the dreams. They diminished in time, but they never left him.

In the beginning, the nightmares were not dreams; they were his life.

Pedro and his sister Maria, two years younger, grew up outside Phoenix, Arizona. Their parents had made their way north when the two were babies, leaving the rest of their extended families behind in Mexico. Given that Pedro's parents were both the weakest link in otherwise stable families, their coupling and travel north did not bode well for future happiness. In Arizona the family settled into a derelict house on the poor side of a poor town.

Pedro and Maria's parents were soon overwhelmed with life and, not surprisingly, their children suffered on a daily basis. Ramon Sanchez took to drinking early in life and when Ramon was drunk he was ugly. Particularly after he wrecked the foreman's truck, he found it hard to get a steady job, so he could be found drinking more days than not. Inebriated, he lashed out in anger often enough to keep his family on high alert. Rita Hernandez, the children's mother, was a woman without any natural spunk, who dabbled in a lackluster manner at life when sober, and found alcohol a welcome escape from all she couldn't manage. She worked when she could, going from farm labor job to maid job, eventually being fired from one after another, generally for not showing up. From the sagging sofa where she spent the majority of her time, she was too often useless for either childcare or child defense. From their tender years, Pedro and Maria cared for each other and for their younger siblings, and for the most part became adept at dodging the blows of their father.

As a little boy, Pedro would climb the lone tree in the back yard to escape from his father and the ever-present need to take care of the younger children. Sometimes he even needed to leave Maria behind and climb the tree. She didn't like heights and would not follow him there. She had her own hiding places. From the branches of his tree sanctuary, he could look down into the neighbor's yard and into the windows of their home.

Reflecting back, Pedro was certain that, without the neighbors, he would have turned mean himself or drowned in despair. Maybe died. The Gonzalez family was not wealthy. No one was in their neighborhood. But the Gonzalez family represented heaven on earth to Pedro, who perched on his branch, practicing being invisible while soaking up what he could of another culture, the culture of a happy family. He spied at them through their open windows as if his life depended upon it.

The father laughed loudly when he got home from work, drawing the whole family into his boisterous orbit. The mother always seemed to be in the kitchen, and the smells of her cooking made Pedro's stomach clench with both hunger and longing. Besides the father and mother, the family consisted of several older brothers who seemed supernaturally tall and strong as they kicked the soccer ball in the street, and many sisters, who all looked pretty and flashy to the boy who saw little of brightness in his own home. There were several ancient men and women who spent their summer days sitting in the shade, constantly attended by the rest of the clan. Children ran into the Gonzalez house and out into the yard. Pedro could not figure out who belonged to whom. Were they the children of the family, cousins, grandchildren? It didn't matter. They had the confidence of children who belong, who are safe, who are cared for. Everything Pedro was not.

Often on evenings when the blazing sun had set and the evening air became balmy, the Gonzalez family would bring their food outside and eat on big tables in the back yard. One night, a young boy came to the fence and looked up into the tree in Pedro's yard. He looked right up at Pedro. His look was neither friendly or challenging. Clearly he had been dispatched on a mission.

"Mama says to come and get something to eat."

Pedro sat frozen on his branch. Fear made him unable to move.

The boy repeated the command, and when Pedro didn't move, he shrugged and moved on to play ball with another boy. Soon he was replaced at the fence by the mother. Señora Gonzalez gazed up at Pedro, who had until that moment held the notion that he was unseen on his branch. She smiled at the little boy, who was shivering despite the warm night.

"Mijo. Come here. I have a tamale for you."

She held up two corn tamales, still steaming hot. Tamales! And it wasn't even Christmas! The smell almost made Pedro swoon. But it took three more invitations for him to move his body slowly down the tree. He looked over his shoulder at his house, but it was quiet.

Señora Gonzalez leaned over the low wooden fence and encouraged him. "Here, mijo. We have so much extra. Would you like one?"

Pedro stared at her hungrily and then held out his dirty hand for the food. He would go find Maria and share it, he thought. Señora Gonzalez gave him both of the tamales.

"Give one to your sister. Your name is Pedro, right? And she is Maria?"

Pedro could only nod. She continued as if he had spoken in full. "Come by the house sometime, I have some clothes my little ones have outgrown that might fit your little sister and brother."

Señora Gonzalez put her hand out to tousle his hair, and he flinched. The look on her face both hardened and softened at the same time. She said something he could not understand, under her breath, and then said directly to Pedro, "You will come, sí?"

Pedro nodded again. He clutched the tamales and turned to go find Maria, and then he stopped, knowing instinctively that something was required of him. He turned to look at her. Señora Gonzalez was watching him tenderly. He said, for the first time in his life, "Thank you. Gracias." And then he ran back around the shed to find Maria in her little hiding spot.

It was the best tamale, the best food, he had ever eaten in his life. He was six years old.

When Pedro started grade school in the segregated elementary school, he got to know Mateo Gonzalez and in time they became best friends. They were as close as two boys from such different homes could be. Pedro could not explain the hell he lived in, and Mateo had no way of asking. Pedro always felt more gratitude than envy, and Mateo was not one to gloat, so the friendship became a life-line.

Pedro's other life-line was Mrs. Harper and her public library. She was incredibly old from Pedro's perspective. She had no patience with trouble makers, and if he was well-behaved she harbored no prejudice because he was Mexican. Her small realm became a haven for the young boy. His sister came with him occasionally, although Maria more often bore the burden of caring for the little ones in the family and could seldom leave the house.

In Mrs. Harper's library, Pedro became lost in the picture books, lapping up the stories and colorful illustrations as an entrance into a wonderful mesh of interesting people and exotic places. The contrast to his own life made his heart race with excitement and fear, as if he was doing something adventurous, even wrong, by peeking in. As he learned to read in school, he devoured books like he did the food he haphazardly received. Mrs. Harper never said kind words to him. She was not glamorous, and she did not smell particularly nice. She did not even go out of her way in the beginning to welcome him. But when she saw what a voracious reader he was, she began providing special books for him, and answering the questions that were coming to his cautious but burgeoning mind. In Mrs. Harper's library kingdom, he could almost forget who he was and how he lived.

One day when Pedro was about ten, he came home from the library in a dreamy frame of mind. The book he had been reading about the ancient world of Greece filled his imagination, and so he was not as alert for danger as he usually was. He saw Señora Gonzalez watering her flowers in front of her home and returned her friendly wave, moving the five books he was carrying into his other arm to lift his hand.

Then the boy entered his home. One step inside the door and the blow landed without warning, knocking him to the ground. A stream of curses followed the blow and carried out the open door. Pedro struggled to his feet. He saw his mother lying on the sofa, a far-off look in her half-shut eyes. His dad lunged at him again. This time Pedro managed to dodge and almost got away, but he tripped on one of the library books that had gone flying when he was first attacked. As Pedro lost his balance, his father, whose rage had escalated while his voice rose even louder, circled his arm around Pedro's neck, holding him up off the ground in a choking grasp. As his feet frantically pedaled in an attempt to find the floor, Pedro smelled alcohol, sweat, and cigarettes, stale and pungent. His father's heavy breathing and the heat from his body dominated Pedro's whole existence in those minutes. That and the vise that was squeezing the breath from him.

As his father squeezed him even tighter, Pedro saw his sister Maria staring at him from her hiding place behind the kitchen door. Her face was terrified.

And then, right before he passed out, when his world became a swirling blur of colors and movement, the front door flew open and his savior stepped inside.

"You bastard, let him go or I'll take your head off!" thundered Joaquin Gonzalez. On either side of their neighbor stood his two oldest sons, as tall as their father now, like silent guards ready to battle.

Even in his drunken rage, Ramon Sanchez was shocked by the intrusion and loosened his grip on his son, who started to slip down to the floor.

"All the way!" barked Joaquin, face red with fury.

And Pedro was released to fall to the floor, holding his chest and neck with both arms in a self-wrapped hug. Tears came to his eyes and rolled silently to his shirt. Besides his relief at having a protector for the first time in the person of Señor Gonzalez, Pedro was grateful that his friend Mateo was not there to witness this humiliation.

Joaquin Gonzalez seemed to understand that shame. He turned to Pedro and said, "Pedro, you and Maria go upstairs to the little ones."

Pedro, staggering to get his balance and breath back, moved quickly. On his way he grabbed two library books that were in the path to the stairs. The others were on the far side of his father and he dared not try to retrieve them. Even at this moment, he felt the weight of responsibility for those books. What would Mrs. Harper say?

Upstairs, Pedro and Maria took the babies into the far room and closed the door, putting a chair in front of the door knob. Pedro never knew exactly what their neighbor said to his parents. But, although Ramon was very drunk, Joaquin got the point across that he would be watching him closely in the future. While Señor Gonzalez had words he wanted to throw at the children's mother as well, he held his tongue. He would let his wife dish out the needed tongue lashing to this poor excuse for a mother.

The Gonzalez family loved family first and foremost, and while there were no saints in the large extended family, contrary to young Pedro's exalted opinion, they were people who would never hurt each other, ever. And the years of watching from next door how the Sanchez children were mistreated had grated on their sense of justice. When Señora Gonzalez saw her earnest little neighbor walk into his front door, library books in hand, and then heard and partially saw what was happening, she summoned her husband and older sons and gave them no choice. Intervene or don't come home for dinner. She wisely held young Mateo back, although he wanted to go along to rescue his friend and help his dad and brothers in this exciting mission.

Knowing they were being watched after that day, the Sanchez parents did try to be better caretakers of their children for a while. But, although Pedro and Maria felt less abuse, they had no trust, and it did not take long for their parents to once again start hitting the bottle. The children continued to be watchful and wary, even though Pedro was never again subject to quite such a raging attack.

And so the Sanchez family stumbled along, the general misery of their lives occasionally modified with more benign days. Pedro's parents made just enough money to buy food in a hit-and-miss manner but not enough to properly feed the growing family. Another baby was born, but Maria and Pedro somehow managed to go to school and take care of the little ones during the interludes when their parents were incapacitated. As they grew, both siblings worked in the fields or wherever they could find work to buy food for their younger brothers and sisters. Perhaps most remarkably, Pedro thrived in school despite the often low expectations some of his white teachers had for Mexican American students in the newly integrated high school. Despite the strikes against him, Pedro won his teachers' support through his effort and love of learning. Maria was probably a bright child as well, but many days she was forced to miss school to tend to the babies as their mother faded into lassitude more and more often.

By 1941, Pedro Sanchez and Mateo Gonzalez were seniors in high school. Mateo excelled in sports, but it was Pedro's tutoring help that got him through his classes. The two boys played in the school band, and were taught to play guitar by Señor Gonzalez, who was part of a mariachi band on weekends. In late spring, Pedro was named the first Mexican-American student in that small town to earn the role of valedictorian.

Graduation was to be a grand day. For weeks Pedro tried to keep his parents happy and away from the bottle so they could attend the graduation and the party the Gonzalez family was throwing afterwards. He thought he had been successful, but when he looked around the crowd as Pomp and Circumstances accompanied the seniors to the stage, he could not find Ramon or Rita. Only Maria was sitting there in her brand new dress, her pride and joy. It was the dress for which she had saved her earnings over the past six months, and she looked transformed. Bright blue, it fell gracefully over her suddenly shapely sixteen-year-old body, and her hair glistened in the new roll her friends had helped her style. For a moment Pedro was taken by surprise. His sister had been his partner in fear, in survival, in hard work all these years. He realized in a flash that she had grown up. When and if he went to college, he would miss her. He felt a lump in his throat, but it was his time to speak and so he did; it was a fine 1942 graduation day speech. War was seething around the world with Pearl Harbor six months past, and he would be drafted now that he was eighteen. His graduation speech was well received, and Pedro felt a glow of having prepared his words and delivered them to the mixed group of students, parents, and teachers sitting attentively in front of him.

The rush of adrenalin after his speech was almost as satisfying as playing in a band. Mrs. Harper was in the audience, a faint but noticeable smile on her face, and Pedro's teachers proudly looked up at him as he spoke. He admired his high school teachers; they were his role models and his heroes. They were symbols of education and culture. In this hot, sparsely populated corner of mid-twentieth-century America, they represented the sanctuary of learning and the promise of new worlds yet to be discovered. It was on his graduation day that Pedro solidified his dream of becoming a teacher himself.

After the ceremony there were well wishes from all sides. Maria came up to him and beamed.

"I'm so proud of you, brother," she whispered to him.

"Maria, I did it!"

"You were magnificent!" Her eyes were gleaming and she lapsed into Spanish. "I am so, so, so proud of you."

"Thanks, Maria. And you look beautiful. That dress is the cat's meow!"

Maria shyly bowed her head. She was not accustomed to compliments and felt both pleased and confused by even her brother's attention.

"You look real spiffy yourself. This is your day, Pedro," Maria replied.

"But, Papa and Mama didn't make it."

"I thought they were going to come, Pedro. I did. I'll run home and see what happened. Need to check in on the babies anyway, just in case, you know . . . ."

She didn't need to finish the sentence, because they both could picture the situation at home. The "babies" were not babies anymore, but Maria and Pedro still felt a responsibility to make sure they were safe.

"Maria, if you wait I'll go with you," Pedro said. "I just need to get my photograph taken with Mateo first."

"Oh no, Pedro. You stay here. It's your graduation, your party. You have to stay. I'll go."

"Okay, Maria, but you must come back. I don't want you to miss the party. The band is playing and you can dance. I'll find some nice boy you can dance with tonight!"

Maria blushed and actually giggled, not something she had had much occasion to do in her life, then gave Pedro another hug and turned to leave. As Pedro watched her go, he saw a couple of high school boys looking at her walk by. Something stirred inside of him. Now he had even more protection to do.

Pedro's thoughts were interrupted when he was swept up into an exuberant hug by Señora Gonzalez who had finally found him.

"Pedro! My little man! You were fabulous!! I couldn't believe that was our little boy all grown up. You're so handsome, and so smart. Oh yes, the words that just came out of your mouth, like a movie star . . . " and on and on she gushed, giving Pedro what he could only wish came from his own mother's lips.

Soon Pedro was caught up in the festivities of his classmates and went on to the party being hosted by the Gonzalez family at a local park set up with balloons and lights and a stage for the band. Food and drink flowed in abundance. How the Gonzalez family would pay for this feast was not an issue that night, nor was their capacity to share their happiness with the boy from next door, now the young man who had made them so proud earlier that evening. Pedro was pulled in to play with the band song after song, and never in his life had he been happier. Behind his celebrating, he felt his future beckon brightly, despite the war.

After a few hours, Pedro became aware that Maria had never shown up at the party. Telling his hosts that he was going to go get Maria and would be right back, he walked the mile home to his house.

Maria had gone home as she said, and sure enough her mother was passed out on the sofa, and her siblings wandered around unfed and trying to scrounge something to eat. Maria flushed with disappointment and anger. It was hard to reconcile the home scene with what she had experienced that evening, sitting in her new blue dress, feeling grown up for the first time, watching her brother be the center of attention as he gave a speech that people listened to attentively and then applauded with vigor. Her brother! Her very own Pedro! And now she came home and saw this. Nothing had changed here. She softened as she witnessed her "babies," as she still called them, at loose ends once again. She was about to take them to the kitchen when she heard a commotion outside and realized her father was returning, not alone, with loud drunken voices announcing the men.

Quickly she ushered all the young ones upstairs out of the way. She heard her father's voice and that of other men. She could tell they were depositing her father on the second sofa, and she thought she heard them leave. If both her parents were passed out, she could go back to the party, and bring back some food.

She straightened her skirt, smoothing the silky fabric down her developing hips, and put a hair back in place. Her brother, Juan, a shy boy of ten, said to her, "You look so pretty, Maria."

"Thanks, mijo. You all stay quiet, stay here. I'm going back to the party and will bring back some good food. Pedro said there was going to be all kinds of special treats. La torta! Ummmm, so good."

The little ones looked at her with shining eyes, anticipating a rare taste treat. Maria always came through for them. She blew them kisses and shut the door carefully to discourage them from leaving the bedroom, then made her way downstairs.

When she arrived in the living room, Maria heard her parents already loudly snoring, splayed unconscious on their separate sofas. She stepped quietly around them, then she shrieked when a hand grabbed her from behind. One of her dad's drinking buddies was still in the house.

"Where ya think you're going little miss?" His grip was tight despite his slurred words. "Hey Stan, Jess, look who's here . . . looking all grown up."

Two other men came back into the house from the porch and leered at Maria who was trying to pull her arm back from the strong grasp that held her.

"Looks like a Mexican whore to me. And what do we do with whores?"

Her parents were too drunk to wake and so did not bear witness to the brutal rape of their sixteen-year-old daughter. Three men, right there on the floor of the living room of that sad house.

Hearing her cries, only young Juan bravely left the others upstairs with a warning not to move and crept down the stairs. What he witnessed froze his small body in fear, and so he did nothing to try to save his sister. Years of hiding from violence, of being shepherded around by this very sister to avoid being hurt, seemed to make it impossible to know any other course of action except to hide and hold his breath.

But holding his breath did no good. His sister was beaten and raped, her beautiful dress ripped to shreds, and her body too. The only good news was that she passed out at some point.

When the men had exhausted themselves, they staggered out the door, putting distance between them and their deed. Maria lay still for a long time. Her younger brother, sure she was dead, finally moved himself back up to the bedroom and crawled under a blanket where his siblings had fallen asleep, still hungry.

Maria came to consciousness. When she remembered and felt the pain of her body accompanying her brutalized emotions, she slowly moved into a crawling position, every move causing agony. In dull motion, she crept into the bathroom, pulled herself to standing and looked at her swollen face in the mirror. She let her eyes travel down her body only in the mirror, keeping herself one step removed from looking directly at the bruising of her body and the violation of her soul. The empty shell of a girl looked back at her. There was nothing left. Nothing left to fight with. She stood there for some time in the silence of the house, hearing only the loud snoring of her father, sometimes joined by her mother's heavy breathing. It was perfectly quiet upstairs. Outside she could faintly hear party-goers at one or another graduation party across town. Occasionally a loud laugh or some music would rise above the general hum of festivities before fading back into the communal noise. A motorcycle sped by. A dog barked. She heard each sound distinctly and amplified.

She thought of her proud brother on his glorious night, and then of her own shame. She felt she had no choice. Her life was ruined. No sense ruining his, too.

She found Pedro's razor in the cabinet. A small scrap of the blue dress still hung at her waist, and she touched it tenderly. Then she climbed into the bathtub.

Pedro found her. He never forgot that he hadn't arrived in time.

Right after the funeral, Pedro and Mateo enlisted in the army. The war was in full force and no one questioned that two eighteen-year-olds would fulfill their patriotic duty and join up, not waiting to be drafted. The Gonzalez family was shaken that their youngest son would follow his older brothers into the war. First this terrible war, and now the losses became personal. Starting when sweet Maria Sanchez was raped and committed suicide, life took a pivotal turn towards harshness, for everyone, even for the Gonzalez family.

At the train station in Phoenix, Joaquin and Esmeralda Gonzalez kept their arms around both boys as long as they could before they had to board the train for basic training. Señora Gonzalez was heaving with sobs. Joaquin was teary as well, but kept slapping the boys on the back to give everyone courage.

When the train was almost ready to move and the boys started to pull away from their elders, Señora Gonzalez held them fiercely one more moment, one of them in each arm.

"Oh Mateo, my baby, our Gift from God, I know you will be safe if you stay with Pedro. He's strong, like the rock for which he was named. Like Saint Peter himself. Stay together, mijos. Take care of each other."

Mateo kissed his mother and turned to hug his father before heading to the train. Señora took Pedro in her arms and entreated him, "Pedro. Take care of Mateo. He's not as strong as you. Keep him safe."

Not knowing what else to say, and willing to promise anything to this woman who had become his mother in all but birth, he agreed with his whole heart. "Sì, Mama. I will. You know I'll always take care of Mateo."

The war years were a blur for Pedro. He and Mateo were miraculously able to stay together, and that was at times the only thing that kept him grounded. They bunked together through the unreal days of basic training where it felt like they were in some strange theatrics learning to be soldiers, a role to which Pedro had never aspired. They were together in the early days in England and then in Belgium, and on to Germany. During lulls, Pedro read aloud any book he could find, filling Mateo's ears with stories of history, adventures of another time and place, science and philosophy, all of which took Pedro temporarily out of his war-time life. Then in the last days of battle, when things were almost over for the German army, a bullet hit Mateo. Sniper or stray, they never found out which. After all the shared moments of fear, all the sights of death both their eyes could not forget, all the hours of boredom spent amusing each other with stories and songs, all the plans for the future they had discussed, it was over. Just like that. Mateo Gonzalez died in Pedro's arms; it only took an instant.

Days later, still in shock, Pedro joined his comrades and marched into Dachau and liberated those whose bodies had survived the concentration camp. One horror eclipsed another. But the soldiers were expected to buck up, be strong, think how lucky they were to be alive and on the winning side of the war. Liberate these poor people, then go home and start a new life. You are the victors. Pedro figured it was the best and the only thing he could do.

When he was discharged Pedro went home to Arizona only once. He did not want to go, but he knew he had to see the Gonzalez family. They had saved his life as a child, and now he had an obligation to tell them about Mateo and share the last years and hours he had spent with their son. As he walked up to their front door he felt immensely guilty to be alive, while Mateo, their real son, was dead, never to return to them.

Dressed now in civilian clothes that felt like a costume, Pedro mounted the familiar shabby steps of the Gonzalez home. He did not glance next door to his own house. He would deal with that later. But first this.

The door flung open before he could knock, and three of the Gonzalez sisters shouted their welcome and pulled him into the house. Mateo's father and a brother were sitting in the living room and rose up to greet him. Pedro held out his hand but he was grabbed full force by Señor Gonzalez and embraced in a long, firm hug while being patted vigorously on his back. While caught up in the hug, Pedro looked over the older man's shoulder and saw a gaunt man sitting in a wheel chair, rug over his knees; Pedro almost didn't recognize the oldest Gonzalez son. And then the kitchen door opened and Señora Gonzalez filled the room with her presence. Everyone stood aside so she could draw Pedro into her bosom and hold him for a very long time. He let himself melt into her, and was for a short time the small boy, Pedro, once again.

"Oh, mi Pedro. Mi Pedro." She cried and spoke in a song of Spanish endearments and rocked him as she had rocked her own babies so long ago, long ago when the biggest obstacle she faced was poverty, and she and Joaquin could together keep their family safe from evil and harm. Now? Now it was all different. But Pedro was here even though her Mateo was gone and her Rueben was barely alive. Manuel and Jose had come back, quieter but intact. Each reunion was something to be celebrated.

When she finally released Pedro and wiped her soggy face on her apron, Pedro remembered that he would never be that little boy anymore. He drew himself back under control and took the seat offered to him, the big over-stuffed chair where normally only Papa Gonzalez sat. Now Señora Gonzalez sat on the chair next to him, and Señor Gonzalez sat on the sofa across from him with a son on either side. The three daughters leaned over their brothers, one pushing the wheel chair closer to the others. Several small children lingered in the corners, curious and momentarily forgotten by their elders.

Reuben was back home now, returned from the Pacific minus a leg and emaciated. He was one of the tall strong sons who had stood guard with their father on that day long ago when they had rescued Pedro from Ramon's strangle-hold. Now Reuben felt like half a man, and it would be a long time before he smiled again without a bitter edge. But his family would care for him the rest of his life.

Pedro sat in the familiar room. It was not the same without Mateo here with him. That was all he could think.

Señora Gonzalez squeezed his arm. Looking into the loving, grief-stricken faces of these parents, Pedro was shamed with how he had not fulfilled his promise. He had not been strong enough to save Mateo. That thought had burdened him daily since Mateo's death. Now, here in the Gonzalez couple's faces, Pedro saw something bigger and deeper than he had known possible. He saw that they loved him, that they did not hold him responsible for having survived while their son died, but he was not capable of receiving that forgiveness. Pedro felt unworthy of that grace.

A silence came over this gregarious family, and Pedro began the conversation just to overcome this discomfort. He glanced at Mateo's sisters, pretty and full of life at first glance, but not as young and carefree as he remembered them.

"Sylvia, Genevieve, Leticia! How you girls doing? Are you behaving yourselves?" It was such a banal remark, and so out of place in this moment, but two of the sisters laughed and tossed their hair back, flirtatiously.

Not Sylvia, however. She was the sister who was closest to Mateo in age and in temperament. Her face stayed serious and she just looked steadily at him, and it felt like a rebuke.

To alleviate Pedro's discomfort Señor Gonzalez intervened.

"Pedro, when did you get back to the States? What are you going to do next?"

Pedro turned to his friend's father and numbly responded to his questions, but the whole situation felt unreal. They all knew what he had come for that day, and it wasn't to talk about his future plans. Not yet anyway. It was Reuben from his wheel chair who opened the door for the discussion the family needed to have.

"Pedro. Tell us about Mateo. Tell us everything. It's the only thing we want to know right now. Another day we'll talk about other things."

Haltingly, Pedro told them all of the last years together in Europe, he and Mateo side by side, searching his memory for something light-hearted. Some of his stories were true and he made up a few as well. Finally they had to know. How had Mateo died? Had he said anything at the end?

Pedro looked straight into their eyes and gave a love-filled falsehood back to them. "Mateo said to tell you that he loved you."

In fact, Mateo had been shocked to have been hit. Pedro could see that in his face, and there was only time for Mateo to say to Pedro in Spanish, "Pedro, what happened?" And then he was gone.

Señora Gonzalez smiled slightly, comforted. Her husband wiped his eyes and thanked Pedro. Rueben looked at Pedro and realized he was not telling the truth, but wisely refrained from comment.

There were no more words in the little living room. Heavy breathing and hiccups of unsuppressed grief were the only sound. Pedro had no more he could say. He carried so much sorrow and guilt that he could not stay any longer and watch this beloved family suffer. He stood and made his way to the door. This time the family was dazed enough that no one got up. Belatedly, as he reached the door, Señora Gonzalez called to him.

"Pedro, mijo, thank you for coming. Come back tomorrow, okay? We'll make a big feast and hear all about your next plans. Okay?"

Pedro, paused and looked at her and at the whole family, who looked at him with forced smiles on tear-streaked faces, all but Sylvia who held her face in her hands and was oblivious to his going.

He knew they did not blame him for Mateo's death. He knew that they really did want him to return the next day. And he knew that he would not come back.

"Sì, Mama, Papa. Tomorrow."

Pedro next went over to his own home. He walked in the front door. Rita was leaning on the kitchen doorway, looking the worse for several years of continued drinking in between periods of hard physical labor. She didn't move towards him when he entered. A couple of his younger siblings were standing behind her, shy in front of this brother they hardly knew any more. Ramon was not there.

Pedro stood and looked at his mother, looked around the house, and tried not to look down on the floor where he knew his sister had been raped. His mother finally said, "So, Pedro, are you going to sit down? Your papa will be back soon and you can tell him all about the war."

Pedro glanced at her, and without saying a word, walked back out the door. He spent the evening with some high school acquaintances, but found no pleasure in the talk. He would not go back to his parents house again. And he could not go back to the Gonzalez home, as welcome as he would have been. He just could not bear it. So he took up the invitation of a young woman, a girl named Celina, and went to her house for the night. He slept with her, finding some relief in the temporary oblivion of sex. And in the morning he left town on the first bus, headed north. The GI bill would provide his college education.

Pedro finished his teaching program in two years. The harder Pedro worked, the more he could keep the demons away. But it wasn't always possible. They came in the shape of nightmares. Sometimes it was his father squeezing the air out of his body. Sometimes it was the sight of his sister, his beautiful Maria, with her life blood draining out of her in the dirty bathtub. Sometimes it was Mateo and the look on his face as he took his last gurgling breath. And often it was the mental photos of the strangers, the human beings in the concentration camp. Those images never seemed to fade but he could keep them away during the day time if he worked hard enough, and so he did.

With a teaching credential in hand, he left Kansas where he had moved for school, and took a bus further north to answer a classified ad he had seen in the college's newspaper. The bus left him off at the junction near Pine Junction, Massachusetts, where his new job waited. He would put all the pain behind him. All of it.

And for the most part he did. Only at night did the haunting return. When Pedro proposed to Victoria Lessing, she was swept off her feet by this handsome, talented and somewhat mysterious man who, unlike every other boy or man she had known, had no history in New England. Victoria, a pretty and very competent young teacher, accepted Pedro's proposal and went into her marriage with happy dreams.

But her worries began after they had been married only a short time. A month into their marriage she woke up one night to the sound of Pedro gasping and thrashing in the bed, harsh gibberish coming from his lips. She shook him and he woke up. The look in his eyes was a shock, full of fear and confusion. Because she loved him dearly, she instinctively drew him to her, and after a brief hesitation, he let himself be held and buried his face in her warm breasts. She comforted him as one would comfort a child. And gradually he went back to sleep and she lowered them both to the pillow.

All night she lay there and wondered what had happened. Wondered what it meant. In the morning a weary Victoria gathered her nerve and questioned her new husband. He looked at her sadly but had no reply. All he could say with great politeness was, "Thank you for being here for me." And in the years to come, that is all she ever got from Pedro about the causes of his repeated nightmares.

Pedro suffered through the bad nights, valiantly. Unlike some men in his situation, he possessed a deep repugnance towards medicating himself with excessive drinking. Before rising every morning he said a prayer to guide his focus towards beauty that day. To push away the ugliness, to embrace life, his choice was to fill his hours with those things that represented beauty and vision, the opposite of violence and depravity. He and Victoria made a home rich with music, art, books, conversation, and good food. He doted on his three little girls, naming the first one after his sister Maria, satisfied that his sister would now have a namesake who could blossom in her stead. Cecilia and Olivia followed, one daughter each year. Fathering his healthy bright girls, and providing them a safe educated childhood, filled Pedro with a sense of redemption.

Pedro told his daughters bedtime stories about a brave, heroic boy named Mateo, never explaining the real boy behind the fantasy story. When years later, Cecilia named her first son Mateo, based on her father's stories, Pedro was overcome with surprise and joy, and instantly bonded with the boy. But he never revealed the connection to the real Mateo.

At first Pedro thought often of the Gonzalez family but his guilt remained too powerful for him to return to them. As the decades unfolded it became harder to break the safe and detached routine of his teaching and family life, and eventually he almost convinced himself, during day-light hours, that there was no past, never allowing the visages of his sister, his friend, and the Gonzalez family to stay in his conscious mind for more than a second before pushing them back into their hiding place. Arizona was a whole universe away. It was better to leave the past in the past. That is what he said to himself without any words at all.

Pedro never shared any details of his past with Victoria because he could not bear to contaminate the purity of his new life with his searing memories. He simply could not unload that on his wholesome wife. She rarely asked, his signal for secrecy was so strong. He never stopped to think that this was not fair to Victoria. He did not imagine that these secrets might form an invisible obstacle in the middle of his charming and charmed family life. It would have been kinder and wiser to have opened up the sealed vaults of his memory, but it was not a risk Pedro was ever willing to take.

At least not until Victoria was gone. And that was a long time. After close to six decades of marriage Victoria suddenly collapsed and died. Without her strength to buffer and hold him, with his teaching years behind him, and suffering the effects of age and illness, Pedro's commitment to silence began to crumble. The scenes and the people of his youth and the war rose to the surface, now in his waking hours, too.

Sixty years after he left Arizona, he knew he had to go back home, not to stay, but to visit, make amends if he could, and find some peace. He would ask his grandson,

Mateo, to be his companion. His past would have to come alive, at least briefly, before it could be finally laid to rest. With young Mateo by his side Pedro felt he could stand up to the devastating memories, and try to redeem his conscience before he died. His sorrowful retrospective could no longer be denied. He would go.

2

A CAREFULLY LIVED LIFE

Warren

1962 - 1991

It had not been a law-abiding month for eleven-year-old Warren. His crimes were premeditated and he was guilty as heck. For three weeks he had plotted this Saturday's misadventures, a bold experiment in emulating adult behavior, which necessitated some theft, lying, and general sneaking around.

This was not Warren's normal mode of operating, but he wanted to impress some school mates; and, besides, he was curious about what was so attractive in the adult lifestyle. So far he could not see the appeal. Dressing up in a suit and tie every day, his dad went off to work in an office, came home and smoked his cigarettes with a drink in his hand, sitting in his favorite chair while watching the news, usually complaining about President Kennedy (his dad had voted for Nixon, that much Warren knew). His mom's life also seemed boring by Warren's standards, although she liked the Kennedys. Observing the adults in his life, Warren assumed he was missing something. Hence his crimes.

Every week he had carefully taken one cigarette out of his mother's pack, only one, and only from his mother. His father, a precise accountant, would have noticed one missing. Warren was sure of that. He concluded that if he was forced to be a criminal to reach his desired goal, then he had to be a smart criminal and assess the situation with a clever and observant mind. His father was too big a risk, but his mother would never notice one was missing from her pack of cigarettes tossed on the kitchen table. But to be safe, he only took one each week, looking repeatedly out the window as she hung out the laundry.

Getting the alcohol was trickier. He had to wait until a Saturday morning when everyone was out of the way: Dad playing golf as usual, Mom at her quilting club, Trina out riding her horse with her friends, and Brian fast asleep. Older than him by three years, Trina spent every Saturday on her horse and never returned until dinner, so Warren felt safe from her bossy scrutiny. His brother, sixteen-year-old Brian, had been out late again the night before and would almost certainly sleep until noon. Warren had put his head under the pillow to try not to hear the loud fight between Brian and their parents when he came in at 3:00 a.m. This was becoming a frequent event, but Warren had yet to get used it, or learn to sleep through the shouting.

Ever since Brian had turned into a teenager three years ago, he had completely ignored Warren. Why would this morning be any different? Warren tried not to care about his sadness at this rejection. From Warren's birth until he was eight years old, his brother had included Warren in his life. Warren had taken for granted his brother's protective friendship, but then almost overnight he lost Brian. His older brother was still in the house, but he moved into a room in the attic and it was as if Warren did not even exist anymore. For a year Warren had trailed after his older brother, only to be ignored or told to get lost. Warren learned to be stoic eventually, but the loneliness was always with him.

Now he focused on getting the liquor. From the pantry he took an empty pint jar, one in the back of the pantry cupboard, forgotten until next year's green beans were ripe and ready for canning. Then he hesitated and replaced it to grab a quart jar. It was hard for him to know what size container was right for the occasion, but he decided to err on the side of quantity. Canning jar in hand, Warren slid into the den. His eyes scanned the cupboard and decided once again to pass on his father's golden brown liquor bottles. Too risky. Whatever brew was inside them was very important. It was the first thing his father headed to when he came home from the office. So he went to the glass cabinet that held his mother's stash of liquid entertainment. Three or four bottles sat there. He read the labels. Gin. Vodka. Rum. Another vodka bottle. He knew his mother went to the refrigerator and mixed something into the drinks, but Warren decided to skip that step. Also no ice. He poured several inches from each bottle, mixing them together in his jar. For good measure he splashed in some more, almost to the top of the jar. Then quickly he took each liquor bottle into the kitchen and filled it under the faucet. Not much, just enough to approximate the original level. He was quite proud of the results and he even wiped off the drips. He could not tell the difference. His mother was usually talking to someone when she was mixing a drink, so he didn't see how she would notice either.

Tightening the lid securely, he took the jar to his bedroom and placed it along with the cigarettes behind the suitcase and baseball bats in the far corner of his closet.

The last step was the hardest. He could no longer avoid touching his father's environment. There had been a very pointed demand from the eighth graders, Paul and Rusty.

"Get some girlie magazines. Find your pop's stash." Much to his embarrassment, Warren had innocently inquired what they meant. The resulting laughter had humiliated him to the core of his innocence, but he managed to try to save face, saying, "Oh, I didn't hear you. I thought you said, 'whirly' and I couldn't figure out what you were talking about!" And Warren had laughed a fake laugh to join the boys' ridicule. But all the next week as he went about his school days, he wondered specifically what it was the boys wanted him to procure.

He soon found out, and when he did, he flushed hot. Gaining this knowledge was absolutely accidental, perhaps even serendipitous in its timing. He had gone into the garage to find his fishing pole when he came across Brian and a friend, so deeply engrossed in something in front of them that they did not hear him approach. Warren was close enough to see what they were looking at, a poster in the middle of a magazine. The picture on the poster was of a naked woman. Completely naked. Warren didn't see much, but he saw enough to make him feel very funny inside. And when Brian saw Warren he reacted so angrily it made the whole situation even more disturbing for the younger boy.

"Damn it, Warren, don't come sneaking up on people, punk."

Brian slammed the magazine closed and hid it from his younger brother.

The friend laughed out loud. "Going to pervert your baby brother with your dad's naked girlies?" He seemed to think this was outrageously funny and roared more, and his laughter was cruel.

"Get outa here, punk. And don't go telling Dad or I'll throw all your underwear in the street in front of the school bus."

Warren turned to run out of the garage, but at the door he stopped and glanced back for a second to see Brian shove the magazine into a hiding place behind their dad's tool box. Then Warren turned back and disappeared into the house.

Brian must have assumed that he had sufficiently frightened Warren into silence, or else he simply didn't care that much if he did get caught. Either way, he never said anything more to Warren. That had been two weeks ago, and now that Warren knew what his older companions wanted him to procure as the cost of admission to their friendship, he knew he was going to go back and retrieve the magazine. It was risky of course. He was both trembling at the anticipation of such uncharacteristic behavior, and yet thrilled. He could think of little else, all day long, in class and at home at the dinner table. He looked at his father and wondered at his business-like father keeping magazines with pictures of naked women hidden in the garage. Naked. The very word stirred something shameful and yet exciting inside the eleven-year-old's young mind and body.

He knew he should wait until the last moment because, unlike the cigarettes and the drinks, he would need to replace the magazine so it would not be missed. But now it was the very Saturday morning he told Rusty and

Paul he would meet them under the bridge. Warren got up very early. In fact, he had hardly slept all night. He dressed, grabbed his supplies and tiptoed down the stairs. He had told his mom the night before that he was going fishing with a new friend early in the morning She offered to make him breakfast but he said no, he would make a peanut butter and jelly sandwich and take a banana and that way she would not have to get up so early. He knew that now that he was old enough to be more independent, she loved her lazy Saturday mornings.

This morning, even Trina was not up yet for her riding lesson. The house was unusually quiet. Warren did not remember to grab the banana, so he left with an empty and very nervous stomach. He entered the garage and went directly to the toolbox. Lucky for him, behind the tool box he found not one but three magazines, all with women on the front who wore little clothing. His eyes grew big. But he had a mission, so he quickly stuffed two of the magazines into his tackle box, thinking Paul and Rusty could each look at one and then trade. Warren was a very practical and fair-minded boy. Prudence told him to leave at least one, just in case his dad or Brian came back into the garage to look again. For a very brief moment Warren wondered what his mom thought of all this. The hidden nature of the magazines, the nakedness, the strange looks on the models' faces all made it an unsettling and thus secretive experience.

He was down the block before Warren remembered to go back and take his fishing pole along with him, but finally he was on his way, down the quiet streets of his home town. It was not completely light when he arrived at the old bridge that connected one side of town with the other; the bridge spanned the creek, running low this time of year but one that stormed wildly in the springtime.

Looking over his shoulders in both directions but seeing nothing, he tightened his grip on the tackle box and his fishing pole and scooted and slid down the embankment leading under the bridge. He went cautiously. Sometimes scary folks hung out down under, but today he had the place to himself. There was no sign of the older boys.

Ever since Warren had been born, his brother Brian had been sufficient for Warren in terms of friendship. Not a gregarious boy by nature, Warren did not seek out neighborhood kids to play with, and even when he entered school, he was content to mix with others but he never got close to the boys in his class. He was not a misfit, just slightly aloof, but never enough to stick out, and no one expressed concern for Warren's lack of friendships. He knew how to maintain a careful life at school, and he simply felt no inclination to make new friends. Brian was all he needed. When Warren got home from school every day, he was included naturally in all of Brian's activities even when Brian's friends were around. Brian was generous with his friendship to his little brother.

And so it was, for the first eight years of Warren's life. Then abruptly, or so it seemed to the younger boy, Brian changed and no longer wanted Warren around. At the same time, Brian also began to argue loudly and frequently with their parents. Everything in the household changed. Warren did not attempt to make friends at school. He only wanted things to be the way they had always been with Brian. Naively, he thought if he waited long enough, life would become normal again and Brian would return to him. But, by age eleven, Warren was beginning to understand that it would never happen.

Warren had run into Rusty and Paul one day while he was fishing by the creek, and while their overtures were not exactly warm and welcoming, for the first time he wanted to impress his peers and be accepted. They lay down their demands for including him in their Saturday activities. This morning's rendezvous was the outcome.

Both nervous and excited, Warren threw some stones into the creek for awhile, hoping to look cool when the boys arrived. But finally, after about a thirty-minute wait, he grew tired of that and sat down with his back against the cold side of the bridge, his tackle box between his knees and his fishing pole by his side. Time went by. Warren had forgotten his watch, a gift from his father last birthday. It felt like hours passed, and indeed he was correct. He thought about leaving but he had planned and worked so hard in this endeavor that he was loathe to go, sure that as soon as he left, the boys would come. They had not specified a time anyway, only saying "Saturday morning."

Warren fell asleep, but a sharp kick to his shin woke him up. He was disoriented for a moment and then the next sensation was that he was intensely hungry, not having had any breakfast. Finally he looked up and saw Rusty was standing over him with a leer on his face.

"Hey kid, got the stuff?"

"Oh yeah, sure, yeah, in here." Warren started to stand up but was shoved back down by Rusty who sat down next to him. Paul crouched on the other side of him and they both looked at Warren with a glint in their eyes.

"Okay, so show it to us. Whatja bring?"

Warren opened his tackle box and pulled out the smokes first, three of his mother's menthol cigarettes carefully wrapped in a tissue. They lay there like jewels in the palm of his hand, and for a short second he felt like a king.

"Menthol Kools! Hell, lady's cigarettes. Couldn't you get some Camel straights?"

Warren was dashed. Was this true? He didn't know. He should not have taken his mom's; he should have risked getting his dad's. However, despite their scorn, the boys grabbed the cigarettes from his hand and pulled out a lighter and lit them. Warren stared, hoping he was going to get to smoke. Finally, Rusty handed him one and told him he could take a puff. Warren tried to do it as he had seen his parents do a thousand times, but he choked, and as he was sputtering, Rusty laughed at him and took it back.

"What else ya got? Got any booze?"

Warren pulled out the canning jar and the older boys laughed so hard at the sight of his container they almost rolled down the embankment into the creek. But they didn't refuse an offer of a drink when Warren took off the lid. They both took big swigs of the mixed cocktail and while they coughed a bit, it was with a swagger and they seemed to be able to handle it. When they put it down, Warren picked up the jar and tentatively took a sip. The older boys taunted him to not be a baby and drink more. So he did, gulp after gulp. It tasted terrible and burned his mouth and throat. His empty stomach received the alcohol without grace. But he was not going to show his pain. He was glad now that he had brought the quart jar so there was enough for everyone. He passed it back and the older boys drank another round and more.

Paul grinned at him, and Warren almost thought it was friendly, although his eyes were blurring so he wasn't sure. "How 'bout the dirty pictures? Did ya get some of your dad's magazines?" Warren wondered how the boys knew his dad had such magazines, but then decided that perhaps everyone's dads had them. There was a lot he had to learn.

He pulled the magazines out. The two older boys lunged for them and each grabbed one. Warren was glad he had decided to bring two.

"So, yeah, you guys can trade when you're done. And then, you know, I'll take them back so my dad doesn't know they are gone." He sounded prim, he realized, but he didn't know how else to speak.

It didn't matter, because Rusty and Paul were too engrossed with the magazines to listen to him. They were grinning and grunting and slapping each other and showing pictures. Warren got a few glances and the views of the women's bodies disturbed him with a new sensation he had not experienced before. His stomach seemed to be lurching, but he wasn't sure if it was the pictures or the alcohol. The older boys didn't seem to be interested in the booze anymore so he took another big swallow, and then another. His head dropped to his chest and he leaned back against the cement wall. Overhead he heard a fast car drive over the bridge. Sometime later there was a siren in the distance. Vaguely, Warren wondered what time it was and what his mother would make him for his Saturday lunch. At some point, he looked up and saw that the boys were leaving and almost out of sight up the embankment, walking away with the magazines.

Warren called after them to bring the magazines back to him, trying to tell them that he would be in trouble if his dad or Brian found them missing. But either they were ignoring him or he really had not formulated his words clearly enough. And then he was alone, under the bridge with his open tackle box, his fishing pole, and a partially empty canning jar of his mother's mixed drinks. Warren was scared and more lonely than he had ever been in his life. HIs stomach felt like someone had gripped it between giant fists and squeezed. To put something in his mouth, he took another drink of the alcohol and then became violently sick.

The quiet underside of the bridge held him as he vomited over and over. Only the buzzing insects witnessed Warren's shameful retching. He lay down on the grass next to his fishing pole, thinking he was probably dying, and fell asleep. Warren slept most of the afternoon, and when he woke up he was still alone. He hurt all over, especially his stomach and his head, and he could hardly move. But he was cold and knew he could not stay there any longer, so he forced himself upright and crawled to his knees and finally to his feet, holding his hand against the cement underside of the bridge. Steadying. Adjusting to being vertical. Finally moving, slowly, so very slowly, he climbed up the embankment, forgetting his tackle box and his fishing pole in the process. It was his favorite pole, another birthday gift. It had been a super birthday. A watch from his father. A fishing pole from his mother. But it seemed a thousand years ago now.

Warren did not see anyone he knew as he took alleys and back roads to get home. If he could have thought of any other place to go, he would have chosen that. But other than briefly considering running away from home to save himself the humiliation that would surely come, he had no thought but to reach his own bed and his own toilet. He was eleven years old and he felt ancient.

Arriving at his house via the alley, he approached the kitchen door as quietly as possible. Coming around the back meant he hadn't seen the sheriff's cars parked in front of his home. But once he was inside the house and preparing to sneak up the stairs, his mother caught sight of him from the living room. She shrieked, "Warren!" and jumped up, ran to him, and grabbed him into a hug. His mother had never been much of a hugger and for years he had received very little touch from her. He was very confused. She did not seem to notice that he reeked of vomit and alcohol. She just squeezed him and cried.

His father was soon beside him too, and Trina. Everyone seemed to be speechless, including himself. Why was Trina not at her riding class? Then he saw through the doorway, two sheriff's officers standing with their caps in their hands, and even Warren's addled brain could see how unspeakably uncomfortable they were to be in the Schumacher living room.

He let himself be pushed and carried into the room but still no one said anything. The silence pulsed loudly in his ears. Warren looked at the sheriff, who finally cleared his throat, and in his official law enforcement voice, altered Warren's life once and for all with two short sentences.

"Son, there's been an accident. Your brother was killed."

In the middle of the circle of his family, with his mother hyperventilating, Trina in a dull stupor, and his father stiffly silent, Warren learned from a stranger that at precisely 12:00 noon his once-upon-a-time best friend and idol, his own brother Brian, had driven across the very bridge under which Warren had passed out. Brian had raced out of town, then off the road at 100 mph and smashed the car into a tree. No one else was injured, but because Warren could not be found anywhere, his mother had been under the impression, despite the sheriff's assurances that Brian had been alone, that Warren too was in the car. Her relief at seeing him walk into the house, filthy and smelly, was the only redeeming moment in the horror of that Saturday. Needless to say, his parents did not notice Warren's condition that day, and no one ever commented on the missing magazines or fishing pole.

Life changed dramatically again for Warren; once again, it all centered on Brian. Brian's death was not discussed among the family, however, Warren thought about the accident almost every day, sometimes grieving the loss of his brother, and sometimes hating his brother for being selfish. His mother, never a warm cozy mom, became perpetually bitter. His father withdrew into his work, and Trina pretty much lived with her friends or at the stables from that point.

When he went back to school after the funeral and a dreadful week at home, Warren was treated with awe and respect for awhile, like a celebrity. Rusty and Paul never bothered him again. The other students worked with him on assignments and asked him to join their teams with a kind of fascination, like he had some weird celebrity status. But in a few weeks his classmates forgot about Warren's brother's spectacular death, and Warren became just a good but unremarkable student again.

The years passed from middle school to high school. Warren joined the tennis team, winning the state championship. He liked playing singles, competitive and solo. His grades were excellent. From the day Brian died, Warren lived a very careful life, trying to salvage his family and not repeat the lifestyle Brian had lived. He didn't consciously think about it, but it was how he found some solidity in a shaken world.

On the day Warren received his acceptance letter to his father's alma mater, Cornell, he walked into the living room where his parents were having an evening cigarette and cocktail. He showed them the letter and for one evening his family almost seemed happy. His mother put down her glass and gave him a peck on the cheek. His father shook his hand and even patted his back. Mr. Schumacher insisted that they go out to dinner to celebrate. Trina was home from college for the holidays and, much to his amazement, she agreed to join them. For that one evening, his family seemed to forget that seven years earlier on a Saturday morning Brian had staggered out of bed, argued resentfully with his parents, then tore out of the driveway in his father's prized Chevy headed to his own demise. For that one evening, Cornell acceptance papers in his pocket, Warren felt he had healed his family by his hard work and success. It had been a long time coming.

But the euphoria did not last even into the next day. By that afternoon his mother was crying into her gin and tonic while Trina made some snacks, and Warren overheard her telling Trina about where she imagined Brian would have gone to school, what Brian would be doing with his life, how smart her first-born son was, how talented. Finally Trina lost patience with her laments.

"Get over it, Mom! Brian is dead. He killed himself and screwed up this family. Get over it and do something with your life besides drinking and complaining. Think of the rest of us sometime. You make me sick. I'm going back to New York. I'm not sticking around for anymore of your whining."

Trina marched out of the kitchen past Warren and stomped up the stairs to pack her bags. Their father walked silently out the door to his garage. Warren bent his head to the doorframe outside the kitchen and resolutely vowed that, should he ever marry, he would never have ugly fights or disagreements in his household.

He kept his nose clean and his days and nights busy during college, doing very well, only occasionally dating, playing some sports but not delving too deeply into collegiate social life or politics. He graduated with his father in attendance, his mother home with "the flu," and Trina out of the country with a job assignment.

Warren moved to New York City for law school, and during his final year of law school he met her.

He was at a party, not his favorite activity but he owed a favor to a law school mentor and could not say no. Standing on the edge of the group, he found an acquaintance and was discussing last week's Wimbledon action when someone put her arms around his waist from behind and squeezed. His shock was as great as hers when he swiftly turned around and faced the beautiful smile and lush eyes of Cecilia Sanchez. Her smile quickly turned to embarrassed laughter as she withdrew her arms and apologized for mistaken identity.

But she didn't walk away and blend in with the other guests. In fact, she was intrigued by this tall, blond stranger with the striking gray eyes. His very aloofness was very attractive to the gregarious Cecilia. Something about his eyes, not shy, just detached, pulled at her. She felt a pure physical attraction that she had not experienced before. Perhaps it was the suddenness of the meeting, the close proximity, and the unwarranted touch that opened up something in her practical spirit. Whatever it was, Cecilia was, at least temporarily, enchanted.

In turn, Warren was fascinated by this dark-haired vivacious woman who was so full of apologies, yet not at all apologetic. The very unexpected nature of her touch also opened up his heart a crack. Out of habit, he tried to withdraw, yet because of his attraction to her, some part of him pulled her to him at the same time. Being open to that magnetic force, Cecilia followed him into a conversation. Looking back, she recognized that it was mostly her talking and him looking at her. She took that to be listening and perhaps it was as close as Warren had ever come to listening to another person outside of class or work. He was enthralled to be in her presence, but conversation was not his strength, so, he just breathed and gazed at her, occasionally answering her gentle prodding.

He learned Cecilia was an old friend of the hostess, almost finished with her degree in library science, and working as a waitress at the Franklin Club. She had been born and raised in small-town Western Massachusetts, and she loved to sing and read. Undoubtedly he also told her about himself under her questioning, but he had no memory of what he said. They became lovers that very night. It was an impetuous move for both of them, but they were immensely attracted to each other. They found the experience worth repeating.

However, Cecilia and Warren were busy with school, so while their dates continued sporadically over the next months, no commitments were made. She remained entranced with his physical presence and was certain that there was a soft vulnerable boy inside that she could help liberate. He was head over heels in love with her body, with the sex, and with all that she represented of the female gender. He was also a little intimidated by her, by her confidence and her sense of belonging. It was clear she had love and affection for her many friends, her parents and her family back in Pine Junction, her home town, and he felt like a solitary man by comparison. It was all rather confusing for him, but the physical gratification was like a drug. It always left him wanting more.

One night, Warren was watching Cecilia get dressed. She quickly pulled up her leotards and draped her skirt around her hips. Ten minutes after their love-making, she was already thinking of which bus to catch to get back to her apartment to finish studying for an early morning exam. As she pulled her sweater over her head and Warren watched her breasts disappear under the fabric, he suddenly felt abandoned.

The words came out of his mouth, surprising him almost as much as they surprised Cecilia. "Cecilia. Let's get married!"

She stopped brushing her hair. Motionless, not looking at him, her gaze seemed to be focused on his bookshelf. Underneath his pounding emotions, Warren found himself thinking she looked like a librarian reading his shelves, searching for a particular book.

Finally she turned, brush still held up towards her tangled hair.

"Warren, you've really thrown me. What do you mean? I don't know what to say . . . I mean, this is a surprise. . . I hadn't thought about . . . I didn't expect this." She gave her hair another swipe of the brush. "I guess I'm speechless, Warren. I simply don't know what to say."

Warren was sitting on the wrinkled sheets, leaning forward, hands resting on his upright knees, and looking up at her. "Just say yes, Cecilia. I want you to be able to stay with me and not have to always go back to your apartment. Let's be together."

Unlike his usual stoic face, he looked as sincere and pleading as a young boy.

Cecilia saw that face. For all her gregarious and independent nature, she was also a compassionate person. She felt very confused between what she really felt, and what she thought she should feel and say and do to match Warren's expectations. So she said nothing for many minutes while she continued to brush her hair.

Eventually, she looked at Warren again. He had not moved, although he had dropped his head and was studying the crumpled bed sheets intently. Without coming closer, Cecilia finally addressed him and he lifted his eyes.

"Well, Warren, I really have to think about this. This idea is just so unexpected. I have a big test tomorrow, so let me get past that and then we can talk some more. I need to run now or I will miss the 10:30 bus."

Business-like, she headed to the door, but then stopped and returned quickly to the bed and planted a luscious kiss full on Warren's lips. Before he could reach for her, she was at the door and closing it behind her. Warren sat there for a moment, confused and disturbed. Then he slammed the pillow against the wall and lay back on the bed, half elated and half in unbearable despair.

Her lack of instant delight to his proposal should have been a yellow flag to him, but he didn't know any better. She finally said a tentative "yes," and then a more positive "yes," under the power of his come-hither eyes. But she asked him to keep the engagement quiet between the two of them for awhile with no big announcements until she finished school. She said that she needed to focus on her last term. He agreed. He, too, was busy with his approaching bar exam. The study allowed him some relief from his sexual obsession. Besides her studies, Cecilia was working overtime at the Franklin Club to pay off her tuition and graduation costs. One night Warren gave himself an hour break from his studies and went to the Club just to see her.

The band that night was popular and the club was packed with customers so Cecilia was very busy. She did not see Warren as he watched her move from table to table, her long dark hair flowing down her back, laughing and talking with her customers who clearly appreciated her charm. She was simply working for good tips, Warren assured himself, but as she walked by the stage, the musicians often called out to her flirtatiously.

At the end of a set, she brought a dark-haired singer a beer and Warren found his throat tightening as the man put his arm around her far too long as he reached for a drink from her tray. Cecilia seemed to laugh and take it all in stride, but there was something disturbing to Warren. She seemed to be enjoying herself thoroughly. His own carefully ordered life had never allowed much in the way of carefree exchanges, and he was sweating as he watched his fiancé move in and among the happy crowd. Warren never went back to the Club and she never knew he was there. He noticed that she rarely wore the ring he had given her. "I don't want to lose it or damage it," is what she said, and "I can wear it all the time when we make a public announcement." But he noticed that most women wore their engagement rings everywhere.

The next month was disjointed for both Cecilia and Warren. Busy with classes and work, they saw each other more irregularly and much to Warren's dismay, they never had sex during this time.

Then one evening after Cecilia's graduation, right before Warren's bar exam, Cecilia showed up at his door. She looked as if she had been crying.

"What's wrong, Cecilia?"

Seeing his books and dirty plates and empty glasses spread out over his sofa and floor she stopped.

"Oh, I'm sorry, this is such a terrible time to bother you. Your bar exam is next week, right?"

"Cecilia, you aren't bothering me. I haven't seen you in ages."

She stood and looked at him, her brown eyes brimming with tears. There was no gaiety in her face or voice. He should have reached for her and held her, but he didn't know what to do. He stood rigid and asked her again, "What's wrong?"

"Warren, I have to give you your ring back. It isn't fair to you."

"What are you talking about, Cecilia? What?" His voice went cold with fear. She continued doggedly.

"I'm pregnant." Again, more slowly as if getting used to the reality of the statement. "I am pregnant."

The words slowly sunk in.

"What? How? You always used the pill. Cecilia, you know this isn't a good time to get pregnant. I need to pass my bar and get my first job. What happened?"

Cecilia was silent, and Warren became furious. "How could you do this to me? To us? We have so many plans." Even as he spoke he realized that what he meant was, "I have so many other plans for us." It was too late to retract, to put forth something more diplomatic, because Cecilia heard him clearly.

The look she returned to him was full of frustration. She felt left out, invisible, yet at the center of his rage. In like manner, now she wanted to hurt him. She fired back the truth, a truth she had not been sure she would ever tell him.

"It's not your baby, Warren."

"I don't believe you."

"Warren, I can do the math. Do you want me to lay it out for you?"

Those simple words crushed something tender. He sat down on his sofa pushing books and papers to the floor mindlessly. He looked away for awhile and then he looked straight at her, eyes like steel.

"Whose?"

"Doesn't matter."

"Doesn't matter? Hell it doesn't matter. Whose?"

Suddenly deflated, she answered him only with, "Warren, I'm not going to say. I don't expect you to stand with me, and I completely understand that you'll never want to see me again. Here's your ring. I'm very sorry to have it end this way."

Cecilia took off the engagement ring and handed it to Warren. He stared at it but didn't take the ring.

He was staring into the future and thought about losing her. Loneliness flashed through his body as his mind bitterly contemplated how his carefully-lived life had backfired, not because of his own behavior, but because of someone else's. With that thought, anger rushed through him again. But then he contemplated losing Cecilia, her face and body, and her tremendous energy that helped him sustain some degree of hopefulness inside himself. He felt punched and scared. Hurt. But all he could do for the moment was to sit there absorbing the potential loss.

Cecilia finally put the ring down on the coffee table and walked to the door. She turned to apologize one more time. He stopped her voice with his question.

"What will you do? Are you going to have the baby?"

"I am. I've spent all week thinking about it, and while I know I could, maybe should, get an abortion, my soul says no, that I can take care of a baby and I can love a baby. I'll go home to Pine Junction. My parents and my sisters will help me."

"What about the father?" Warren forced himself to ask.

"He's not connected to me. We're not in relationship, only a one-night stand, a one-night careless stand, but I don't hate him and I don't want to burden his life or complicate mine. So I'll do this myself." Her resolute tone covered the twisted feeling in her gut and the nights of re-crimination and tears over the past week, but Warren only heard her self-sufficient voice.

After she left, Warren sat there surrounded by his books, unable to study, clutching the discarded ring in his palm, opening and closing his hand over its shimmer.

Warren's night was agony but in the end his grief and his need overcame his anger. Early the next morning, he called her.

"Cecilia. Marry me. We'll make it work even if it's not my child."

There was a long pause. "Warren, I'm not sure that's a good idea. It could get very complicated for you. I'm not sure you've thought this out."

"Yes, I have, Cecilia. All night. Marry me. We can make it work. We're both strong people and hard workers. We can make it work. We can have kids of our own later on."

"Warren, I've already decided to go back to Pine Junction. My parents told me that the librarian at our local branch is retiring, and I'm going to apply for his job. My family will help me with the baby. I know you have other plans, elsewhere."

"I'll come with you, Cecilia. I can practice law in your town as well as anywhere. It'll work out. We'll make it work."

"You'll always want to know who my baby's father is. It isn't a good idea." But Cecilia's voice faltered and weakened the resolve of her words.

Warren sensed that Cecilia was weakening, so he pushed on and vowed, "I'll never ask, Cecilia." He repeated, "We can make it work."

In the end, Cecilia agreed to marry Warren. Warren's mother said she would not be able to come; she had never liked the idea of her son dating, much less marrying, someone with a Spanish last name. Warren's father had suffered a stroke and was in ill health. His sister was traveling again. Hearing that Warren's family could not come, Cecilia decided to not invite her family either, choosing a quick wedding with a justice of the peace and two college friends as witnesses.

After they arrived at their hotel room for their honeymoon night, they both lay down on the king size bed exhausted from the combination of exams and stress. Cecilia thought she should try to put on a sexy negligee and make the night special but a bout of nausea overcame her and returning from the bathroom, she gave Warren a weak smile and fell asleep. He watched her for awhile, her dark hair falling across her cheeks and he pulled the covers up over her body, in part as a tender gesture and partly to obscure her body from his need for her.

The very next day Warren and Cecilia moved to Pine Junction. Cecilia, as a returning daughter of the town, was greeted with cries of welcome wherever she went, and she did fall right into the library job. Her pregnancy was not apparent for several months, but when it was, people were even more effusive in their homecoming excitement. Warren, who had just passed the New York Bar exam, now threw himself into studying for the Massachusetts Bar, meanwhile doing legal work for Ralph Taylor, a local attorney. Although he sometimes felt like an outsider in Cecilia's small town, Warren's career took off productively; on that stage, he was always successful. During the months until the baby's birth, Warren convinced himself that he and Cecelia could put the past behind them and make the marriage work. But from the day Mateo was born in January of 1977 and thereafter, he knew the marriage was not working.

Warren had struck out in his relationship, but had no idea what to do. At night he sometimes mulled over what he would like to change, how he could make the situation more satisfying, but he was caught inside his own scars. The barriers seemed unmovable. Cecilia floated miles away and he had no idea how to reach out to her. What rescued him now was his ability to compartmentalize his emotions away from his daily life. It was a temporary salvation to live each day acting as though all was well. He convinced others and, some days, himself.

While Cecilia held her secret close to her heart, sleep-walking quite effectively through her days as she lovingly cared for her baby and worked in the town library, Warren once again crafted a very carefully constructed life. And so their time in Pine Junction began to unfold, day by day. Lifting his champagne glass to Pedro at his father-in-law's 1977 New Year's Eve party, Warren smiled a polite smile to the family and neighbors gathered to welcome in their hope for the new year - 1978. Cecilia smiled too and kissed baby Mateo on his chubby cheeks, while Warren watched her from across the room. Their eyes did not meet, not then and rarely over the next years. They led busy and tranquil-looking parallel lives for many years, while Warren kept the promise he had made to himself long ago; fighting and arguments were not part of his life.

3

ONE EVENING DOES A LIFE MAKE

Dane

1976

Looking up from his guitar one night, Dane spied the new barmaid. He saw her from the back first, and there was something about the way she held herself that caught his eye; he liked how her waist-length black hair was held out of her face by a colorful scarf in gypsy style. When she turned around, just by proximity, her eyes fell right into Dane's gaze. He smiled. She smiled. She went on to her next table, focused on her job. Dane turned back to his guitar tuning, but kept picturing her face and her attitude. He was attracted. Dark brown eyes, as dark as his own. Not Mediterranean like himself. Latina, he guessed. There was something in that brief glance that he tried to put in a category, but he struggled. Hers had not been a flirtatious smile. Not simply business-like either. Not disinterested, but not needy. Composed, but friendly. He couldn't put a tag on her, but he was interested.

Dane was close with the Franklin Club barmaids. The older women had nurtured him when he was underage and very green, and he had friendships with the younger women, each one with a different story behind her employment at the club. But Dane was married to his music and he never put energy into a serious relationship, only into enough flings to be able to pretend he understood his songs of love and broken hearts.

By the mid-1970's, although still a young man, Dane Faber was an experienced musician. He had been playing and singing at the Franklin Club, one of New York City's finest, before he was legally allowed to enter its double front doors. His ageless voice had a plaintive appeal that would grow huskier over the years, and Dane could count on a satisfying following among the Franklin regulars by the time he was twenty-six.

Later that night, Dane managed to pass through the back room where the new barmaid was reading a book while on her break. She looked up and, again, she smiled pleasantly but not invitingly; so, he stopped against the wall and pulled out a cigarette to justify his presence. He asked her if she minded if he smoked. She said yes, she did. The back room was the one place she could get away from the cigarette smoke that hung over the club inside. He put the pack away, having no more use for them now that there was a conversation started. That conversation was about six minutes long before she was called back to work. Still it was something, and finally Dane figured out what had intrigued him. This beautiful woman was not frivolous. In those few minutes she had brought up at least three topics of significance (Dane counted them), spoke knowledgeably, and then listened to his replies with attention. So, that was it. That is what Dane perceived in his first glance from Cecilia Sanchez. Intelligence.

Most of the male patrons, as well as the musicians and bartenders, mooned over Cecilia's physical beauty, but from Dane's perspective, her intelligence was what heightened her appeal. But there was little time to talk. The club was busy and the maids hustled for their tips, while the manager watched her workers like a hawk. The musicians had lives of their own and Dane often traveled to engagements elsewhere in the City and out of town. So Dane just watched Cecilia when he could, and found that under the spell of keeping her a mystery, he was writing some of his best music.

Still, as he wondered about her, he lusted for her, all the while secretly observant for any competition for her affection. She wore no ring, and he never saw her with anyone at the bar or after her shift ended. She was friendly with every customer, but never encouraged any fooling around. Once he saw her firmly remove a lecherous hand from her backside. Dane was angry for her, but when he said something to her later, she just shrugged and told him that she understood the club mentality and that she needed the job to finish school. She seemed touched by his concern but said she could handle it, thank you. Cecilia slipped out of the club every night immediately after her shift, never hanging around to decompress as many of the barmaids did.

When he learned that Cecilia was studying for her library science degree, Dane thought it appropriate. His own education consisted of a high school degree, but he had not stopped school due to lack of ability. He left school solely for his dream of sitting on the stage to tell stories through his music. He was well-read in his own sort of way. His father was a philosophy professor at the State University of New York, therefore Dane grew up surrounded by books. His memories were of kitchen-table discussions with his Cyprian mother, singing and urging him to "eat, eat, before it gets cold," and his more ascetic French Jewish father, winning his attention with "talk, talk." His adored mother died soon after Dane's twenty-first birth-day, after which his father stayed in the same Manhattan apartment, thinner without his wife's good cooking, sad, lonely, but his active mental skills kept him engaged with ideas. Dane dropped in twice a month, bringing food to cook his father a meal. The two would sit around the old kitchen table, and now Dane would tell his father to, "eat, eat," all the while his father would want to just "talk, talk." Dane honored his mother's memory through creative cooking, and his father, by becoming a great listener. It was all fodder for his music, of course.

Nights at the club, Dane was bewitched by Cecilia Sanchez. But without any encouragement, he never asked her for a date. He dreaded the day she would quit the club, as was certain to happen when her degree was finished and she found a library job. She was so beautiful it made him ache. The way she tilted her head when memorizing an order from a crowded table. The way she smiled at her patrons without giving any of herself away. The way she glided through the crowded tables like grace itself. The sway of her hips created an elegant rhythm and as he watched her, right in the middle of a song, Dane would find himself getting extra husky. Little gestures tugged at his senses: seeing Cecilia run her fingers through her hair as she stood by the bar waiting for an order to be filled, her eyes half closed in contemplation of some unknown thought. When someone would speak to her, a lovely smile would again appear. Occasionally her friends would come into the club for the evening and she would greet them

with a hug and cheek kiss, exchange some short conversation, and then be back to her waitress duties with an
always-professional smile.

Dane thought of inviting her to take a walk after the
night's music was done - what could be so difficult about
that? But she always slipped away. He thought of calling
her at home, but he would have to go through devious
means to get her phone number and his lust felt private.
He longed to not just sleep with the elusive Cecilia, but to
stay up all night talking to her. He even had the fantasy of
bringing her to share a dinner-time conversation with his
father, convinced that his father would love her, and that
the talk would be stimulating. Granted, he based this on
very little actual knowledge. It was just an impression, fueled by his yearning.

Cecilia worked at the Franklin Club over two years before completing her degree. From a casual remark, Dane
realized one night that her time at the club was soon to
end. He felt a sense of panic. It was the night before his
band was to launch a six-week tour of the Midwest, a trip
Dane anticipated with mixed feelings because he never enjoyed road trips. At the break between sets, he sat onstage
replacing a string on his guitar when Cecilia brought him
a drink. The club was full to bursting that night, and the
energy and noise was a roar around them. Smoke filled
the air above and swirled around them; to his mind, he
and Cecilia were in an isolated bubble as she stood next to
him. He felt her physical closeness as never before, and it
felt natural to put his arm around her waist as she handed

him the drink and, when she didn't pull away, he pulled her in a little closer, not too much, just enough for him to breathe in the scent of her body, a slightly sweaty smell mixed with sweetness, not cloying but rather earthy and intoxicating to Dane's wide-open senses. The good fatigue of an evening of music added to his reduced inhibitions. Perhaps something of the night had rubbed off on Cecilia too, because she relaxed into his hug for a few exhilarating moments and lightly placed her hand on his shoulders as his arm encircled her waist. Her breasts were about level with his eyes as she stood next to the stage where he sat, and he soaked up the sight of their roundness just above the neckline of her low-cut peasant blouse.

Before his courage left him, and with his arm still around Cecilia's waist, he asked her if she would wait for him after the evening's music. Given her past history of slipping away after work, he could only hold his breath, but, much to his amazement, she said yes. He looked at her face and tried to determine what she was thinking or what her expectations were, but he could not read her mind behind the warm brown eyes and flushed cheeks. However, she was smiling and she had agreed to meet him. He would enjoy his hope for the duration of the next set.

And after he packed up his guitar and waved a quick farewell to his band mates, ignoring their calls to join them to discuss their upcoming travel, he rushed off through the kitchen and bumped smack into Cecilia who was sitting on a stool with her bag over her shoulder and a book in her hand, waiting. He grabbed her hand and pulled her outside. He had her to himself! She was up for a walk, yes, that would feel good. So they walked, and he asked her about her studies and plans. She confirmed her graduation coming in a few weeks, and a couple of jobs she was applying for, both of them in New York, which Dane was happy to hear. He asked her more about herself and she told him her home town was in Western Massachusetts, that she had two sisters, her parents were high school teachers, and she liked to sing.

Dane asked her why she never came up to sing with them on stage. She smiled and demurred. Thinking she was just shy, Dane pursued it, having flash fantasies of Cecilia on the stage with him forever. She finally admitted that her singing experience was more classical. She had started singing in the church choir, and from there she sang in concert choirs in college, and in festivals, and she hoped to do it again. While the Franklin Club had provided good money for her, she would be glad to get away from the smoke, which had not helped her voice. She wondered how he could take it. He responded that his voice was kind of husky anyway. She nodded. He wondered what that meant. He wondered what she thought of his singing, of his whole life's passion.

He thought about mentioning that many great folk and rock singers began their musical life with classical music training, but decided that the conversation should shift in a less controversial direction. He was positively jangling walking beside her down the crowded post-midnight streets, and he let his arm press against hers as they made their way. She was still clad in her barmaid outfit but the night had turned chilly. He saw her shivering and he draped his jacket around her shoulders. He was rewarded with a beautiful direct smile and it gave him courage to ask her if she wanted to stop by his place for a nightcap or to smoke a little grass. Not expecting her to agree, he was thrilled when she gave only a second's hesitation and then said sure.

Walking on air, he turned the next corner onto the block where his apartment was. His was a five-story walk-up. By the time they got to his floor, they were both panting and it seemed to put them into an even softer mood. He unlocked the door and motioned her to enter his studio apartment, being glad he had washed his dirty dishes before he left that afternoon.

Cecilia took off Dane's jacket and gave it back to him, thanking him for his gallantry. He tossed it on the chair and asked her if she wanted a drink or some grass. Again, she seemed to pause only slightly before she said she would smoke a little something if he had it. He did. Not much. He was not a heavy drinker or smoker, but liked a little toke now and then to unwind. A band member kept him stocked for his minor needs. Like right now, he thought.

He led her to his couch and swept off some books and music and clothes. She sank gracefully into the cushions and pulled up her legs on the length of the couch and stretched her arms up in a gesture she may have done every night when she got off work, but now in his little studio, it felt to Dane like a very intimate gesture. He gulped and retrieved a joint and a match and came over to join her. He sat down on the hassock next to her so he could soak all of her in with his hungry eyes. He lit the joint, and passed it to her first. Again she smiled and called him a gentleman before taking a practiced inhalation and holding it in, then she passed the joint back to him. He did the same, and back to her, and back to him. But, on the third time when he passed it to her, she declined, gave him a languid look, saying that a tiny smoke went a long way with her. That she had learned that the hard way back in undergrad days.

He, too, put away the joint in the ashtray and asked her if she would like a back rub. Yes, there was nothing she liked better and she easily rolled over on the couch. Touching her back through the gauzy peasant blouse was an escalating thrill to him, but the cloth kept bunching up under his hands, making it natural to pull up the shirt and place his hands on her bare skin and work her tired muscles with his own guitar-calloused fingers. She sighed with pleasure. Well, who doesn't like a back rub? But Dane felt it was because his hands were giving her intense delight and he could have kept doing this for the rest of his life. At some point in this magical time, he lifted her blouse up and over her head. She raised herself up to help him and from above he got a quick sideways glimpse of her breasts before she lay down again on her stomach. She stretched her arms up to circle her own head and hold her hair out of the way, and the elegant arch of her back lay under his hands that rubbed her skin, a warm brown color that matched his own. As he worked his fingers over Cecilia's back, he could not take his eyes off the rounded sides of her breasts pressed into the old chenille sofa. At some point he took his own shirt off and lay his chest down on her back, feeling the electricity of contact, skin to skin. His lips nuzzled into the nape of her neck, kissing and nibbling and letting her luxurious hair tickle his face.

She was breathing deeply but not sleeping. When she started to move he lifted his body up but all she did was roll over under him on to her back, a sight that sent electrifying waves up and down Dane from head to toe. For a moment he could only stare at her before reaching to hold the fullness of her breasts in his suddenly-trembling hands. Cecilia put her hands on his face, and then tangled her fingers in his hair pulling his lips down to hers. For at least that moment, he knew she wanted him, and she was the only one he had wanted for two years now.

But then she stopped and cried out in vexation at herself. Her pills. In the busy countdown to her finals she had not picked up her prescription and she was completely without birth control. Dane thought he would burst at stopping their love-making because her desire for him had overtaken whatever self-control he possessed. But he honored her; her presence commanded honoring and he would stop. He would. He asked her if she wanted to stop. She said no, but that she had to. Then she asked him if he had a condom. It took him less than three seconds to find one in the back of his drawer. He knew it was old. He knew it was suspect. He knew it. That is what he remembered later, years later. But at that moment he was willing to take the gamble. What were the odds anyway? The only thing that mattered was that moment. Having her. Giving himself to her. Sharing their bodies.

Consummating that evening was as exciting as the anticipation. That had not always been the case for Dane in his love life. Nor would it be in the future. This was the night he would recall for many years. The shining night he held as a standard with which to compare subsequent encounters.

They lay there afterwards on the old couch, comfortable with their nakedness, talking. And for an hour, maybe a little more, Dane felt he had everything. Incredible sex with this amazing woman, and now, the conversation he had long imagined, although he was glad his father was not present as he lay his head on Cecilia's lap and looked up at her breasts and face. They talked of many things, of music and books and places they'd been. Of thoughts and ideas. And families. With warmth she sympathized with him on his mother's death and was interested in the classes his father taught. She told Dane her mother was of New England stock for generations, English and German well back into history. Cecilia's father was Mexican and she knew almost nothing of his background, but she spoke fondly of him. She did not speak of boyfriends, and Dane didn't want to spoil the night by asking her and possibly unmasking a roadblock to his dreams of their future together. At least for tonight, his fantasy could be real. Live for today, he told himself. Dream of tomorrow.

Cecilia left him sooner than he was ready. After an hour or more of tenderness and talking, she sat up and began to gather up her clothes, saying she had to get home because of an interview the next day, not until the afternoon, but still, she needed some sleep before facing it. Sleep here, he found himself begging because his hands didn't want to stop touching her. She said no, it was time for her to go. She reminded him that he had to hit the road early for his band tour. He protested that he could operate on little sleep with no problem. Cecilia firmly replied that it was a problem for her, that she had to go, that she had a lot to do.

Dane told her then that he would be gone for six weeks and asked if he could write to her or call. She replied, matter-of-factly, that she would be moving soon herself and didn't know her new address or phone number. She wasn't cold, just firm, but it felt cruel to Dane. He asked her if she wanted him to walk her home, and she answered no, that she only lived three blocks away. He told her that he thought it was funny that for two years she had lived three blocks away and he had not known. Funny. And, just like that, the night was over. Cecilia left with a kind smile but only a light kiss on his cheek. Then gone.

For the first weeks of his band tour Dane moped, realizing that now he knew what a lopsided one-night-stand felt like from the sad side. One person infatuated, if not in love. And the other, enjoying the delights of one night only without any entanglement.

When he returned from his six-week tour, Dane walked back into the Franklin Club, excitement mixed with apprehension. He stood looking around. The senior barmaid, who had taken Dane under her wing when he was a seventeen-year-old singer, and perhaps the only one observant enough to know of his infatuation with Cecilia, took him aside. Gently she told him that Cecilia was not at the club anymore. She told him what she knew - that Cecilia had married an attorney and left town. Dane's face posed the question. The barmaid shook her head and told him that she didn't know where Cecilia had moved. When Dane didn't respond, she finished the news, explaining that Cecilia had been gone for three weeks now and she was sorry that Dane didn't know. Putting her hand on Dane's arm, she asked him if he was okay. Dane managed a nod without making eye contact with his old friend.

The barmaid squeezed his hand and cheerfully changed the subject telling him that it looked like a good house that night, and made sure he knew that everyone was glad he and his band were back in New York. Dane managed a fleeting smile, so she gave him a further pep talk, telling him how much everyone loved him, how his band was the club favorite. Then she added the news that a new barmaid had been hired. However, her offer to introduce Dane to the young woman was spoken to Dane's retreating figure.

Life goes on. Careers go on. Things can be forgotten. Dane eventually found himself more able to focus on his music and his friends without the distraction of Cecilia in front of his eyes. In time, he kept that one enchanted night as a memory in a corner of his creative mind, using the experience to feed the yearning in his music. It worked well that way, and kept him from dwelling on the loss of what he never possessed. He saw it as maturation on his part; then, finally, he was able to be happy for the rite of passage into a more sane and steady life, which is a relative state of being for a traveling musician. But he never seemed to find anyone else to fall in love with, much less marry. From time to time he was curious where Cecilia had gone and what the guy was like whom she had married. And he sometimes wondered if she ever had any children. Yet, for decades he never pursued his questions.

It was early in 2005 when that all changed. Late one night after a performance in a Seattle club, he felt hands over his eyes and turned around to see a vaguely familiar face. He couldn't retrieve her name, so the somewhat tipsy woman cleared up the mystery for him by repeating her name several times, and finally responding to his still confused face, she said, "New York, Franklin Club, long time ago. I was a barmaid."

Then he remembered her. And in a flash, he remembered that she had worked at the club during the same period as his infatuation with Cecilia Sanchez. Funny how those memories could come hurtling back hard and strong all these years later, almost thirty years he quickly calculated. While he did a very abrupt dive down memory lane, the woman continued to chatter. About his own age, definitely full of cocktails, she grabbed his arm and pulled him to a corner of the bar and offered to buy him a drink for old time's sake. Clearly she was delighted to see him and in a mood to bend his ear.

Politely, he sat down, thinking he would unwind with her for an hour and then head back to his hotel room, alone. Definitely alone. He would have to be sure of that because the old acquaintance, Sandy was her name, seemed to be all by herself and in a sloppy sentimental frame of mind. After years on the road, Dane had learned how to keep his boundaries strong.

Sandy talked on and on about the folks from their mutual past. She had been living in Seattle for over twenty-five years, but seemed to recall her old New York friends clearly; perhaps the alcohol had enhanced her memory for old times. After gushing over Dane and his band for awhile, she suddenly mentioned the very person Dane would never have brought into the conversation: Cecilia Sanchez. He didn't remember Cecilia ever socializing with any of the other barmaids, but it seems that she had, at least to a degree. Sandy began talking about Cecilia's abrupt departure from the club, apparently weeks earlier than her long-stated plan to leave. The manager hadn't been too pleased because it had all been so sudden. "Cecilia's whole personality changed, her whole attitude was different!" Sandy emphasized with bleary eyes but a confidently confiding voice here on this Seattle night almost three decades later. She said all the barmaids thought it was a shame that Cecilia hadn't taken the library jobs in New York that she had applied for, that for months she had made it clear she really wanted to stay in New York, but then, just like that - and here Sandy made an attempt to snap her fingers - Cecilia had to return to her home town because she was pregnant and had married some man that no one at the club had ever met or that she had ever talked about, not even once. Sandy rolled her eyes. Well, it was only rumored that Cecilia was pregnant at the time, but they had all caught her throwing up in the bathroom and one of the barmaids knew an old friend of Cecilia's who later confirmed that Cecilia was working in her home town and had had a baby boy.

Sandy soon slipped into gossip and reminiscences about other old Franklin Club workers and musicians; her memory was prodigious, but Dane did not hear a word more. After some time he called a cab for her and firm-ly settled Sandy inside after she planted a wet kiss on his cheek, missing his lips as he twisted his face. Dane paid the driver, and walked off to his hotel. He had a lot to think about.

When he arrived at Cecilia's front door a few weeks later in the small town of Pine Junction, Massachusetts, he could see how severely he shocked her. If he had not been so obsessed with his mission, he too would have been stunned to be there with her once again. She was so shook up to see him that she confessed to the truth of his sum-mation, and then spent the next ten minutes telling him to leave, which he finally did. For weeks she refused his phone calls, and then before he could decide what to do next, three months later, he returned from a gig to find a message from Cecilia on his machine. Their son had suffered a terrible assault and lay in a coma in the hospital.

His son, Mateo. Mateo bore the last name Schumacher although his parents were divorced. Mateo did recover, and after he recovered, Cecilia finally told Mateo about Dane's fatherhood. As can be well imagined, it took some time to adjust to such news, but Mateo soon allowed Dane into his life. Both were musicians. Both loved living in New York, although Mateo lived in Brooklyn with his girlfriend Catherine, and Dane was on the upper West Side in his father's old apartment. In fact, once the relationship was established, it was relatively easy. Remarkably easy. Mateo had that kind of personality: flexible, open, a believer in miracles and coincidences, and after his injury, grateful to be alive.

After he regained his health, Mateo went to college at age twenty-nine and earned a business degree, which surprised everyone who knew him. Eventually, over thirty years into his long singing life, Dane brought on the thirty-three-year-old Mateo to be his new business manager. And it was at this time, perhaps under the spell of Mateo's golden touch, that Dane found himself enjoying his time on the road, able to relate to musical audiences from a broader spectrum. Finally he was able to relax to the rhythm of America, from Austin to St. Paul to Portland to Virginia Beach. He discovered that there was life that he could enjoy beyond his home city.

Mateo had that charisma with most everyone he met, to help them see the broader picture of life, to open up their hearts to other people and to other places. Of course, he had a particularly powerful relationship with Dane Faber. And this was fitting because Mateo was Cecilia and Dane's son, conceived one romantic New York evening, when the only thing flawed was the condom.

Over time, Dane developed a friendship with Cecilia. Amazingly, it was a comfortable relationship between the two. Cecilia was involved romantically with another man whom she soon married, and Dane found himself without jealousy. It was possibly because of this liberation that Dane finally fell freely in love with a woman who lived in his very own apartment building, and she loved him fully in return. That is another and a beautiful story, just showing that while first loves can carry a powerful oomph, late loves are often the best.

4

THE COOL MR. G

Rowan

1991

Every student at Paul Revere Elementary School - all the boys and all the girls - looked forward to fifth grade. Finally they would be the leaders of the school, and, at last, the lucky ten-year-olds would be in Mr. G's classroom.

Dale Grosnicholas was the coolest teacher in school. This was universally acknowledged by the girls who discussed him either in serious conversations or worshipful giggles, depending upon their maturity. It was also the accepted opinion of the boys, who loved having a male teacher who was athletic, musical, cool, and still gave the students what they really wanted: fairness and steadiness. Some people are born teachers, and Mr. G was a natural.

As for Dale, he considered himself lucky to be able to spend his days with children and with learning. He held other jobs after college and was often bored, but after he discovered teaching he was never bored again. Dale had been a restless young man, but now the hours in the classroom settled him, and the kids made him laugh every day. He genuinely liked his students. Their needs and their education were a sacred trust to him.

Until this week, Rowan Schumacher had loved every minute of his fifth-grade year. An average student and an excellent athlete, he was well liked by his teachers and peers as a team player and leader. Life was good for Rowan.

On this April day however, Rowan sat at his desk with a dark cloud over his head. He stared at his math test, and the concept of negative numbers he had been proud to master last week was incomprehensible today. The test page began to blur, and to his horror his eyes misted over. Humiliated, he tried to subtly wipe his eyes without attracting any attention from his classmates, most of whom were busily filling in their test page.

Rowan would have been horrified to see that the notoriously unfocused Perry Schroeder had noticed Rowan's furtive move to his eyes. Because of the spelling of their last names, Perry and Rowan had been seated near each other from kindergarten until fifth grade. Even those teachers who didn't arrange the students alphabetically often put Perry near Rowan because Rowan could handle Perry's impulsive behavior. Most students were so annoyed by Perry that the teachers soon learned to seat him around the most generous or unflappable students. When Rowan complained about this at home, his mother told him that Perry couldn't help himself and Perry needed friends, too. And so the two boys continued in close proximity year after year.

Fortunately, Mr. G was skilled enough that he could bring out the best in Perry. He had not seated Perry near Rowan all year long, almost as if he knew Rowan needed a break, but after so many years of proximity, Perry seemed to have a beam out on Rowan. Perry, who was seated across the room from Rowan, his desk right under Mr. G's nose, was wiggling in his seat and twisting around, balancing his chair on one of the four legs, his head turned and his eyes on Rowan just as the boy brushed the tears out of his eyes.

For this one rare moment, Perry Schroeder squashed the comment that on any other occasion would have popped out of his mouth. It wasn't that the class was in the middle of a math test that inhibited Perry's comments. Rather it was a combination of Mr. G's close presence and an underlying recognition that this was *Rowan Schumacher* making the blunder of crying in class. Perry held Rowan in the highest regard. Rowan had always included Perry on his ball teams, although Perry swung wildly at every pitch, and, when on the court, Perry never shared the basketball. Even when Perry had knocked over the trophy cart with his field hockey stick, Rowan had stifled his scorn, not joining in the chorus of peer mockery that was Perry's daily fare. Inwardly Rowan was often irritated with Perry, but all Perry knew was that Rowan was one of the few in school who did not make fun of him, and sometimes Rowan even helped him with his difficult subjects.

So now Perry shut his mouth and turned and looked right into the eyes of his teacher. Mr. G's eyes followed where Perry had been staring and he saw the scrunched-up look of sorrow on Rowan's face.

Rowan stared at problem #3, having passed on #1 and #2, but all he could see was the empty space in the driveway where his dad's car had always parked and all he could hear was his mother's voice saying his dad would be living in Amherst. All he could feel was confusion and rage.

For three days now, Rowan had hated his mom with all his eleven-year-old passion. He would not hate his dad. That was not safe. Dad had gone and Rowan needed to keep some hope that his dad would return or that he would ask Rowan to come live with him. Rowan had always loved hanging out with his dad. They didn't talk much, but he loved being in his dad's world - his office, his car, his golf and tennis outings. He needed his dad. And now he was gone. Rowan didn't understand anything about why, but he just knew it was his mother's fault, and he hated her for that and for turning his whole world upside down. He wanted to hurt his mom, to punish her for what she had done to him, what she had done to his dad.

Never before had Rowan hated his mom. Mostly he took her for granted. Mateo hung out with their grandfather and Rowan hung out with his dad. His mom was just there, working in the garden, reading books, going to work at the library, drinking tea, making dinner, driving him to practice, making cookies for him and his friends, just being his mom. But now she had betrayed him, and he refused to remember the games and laughter and story times he had shared with his mom. He didn't dare think that his father had betrayed him, too. It simply was not possible.

Rowan's pencil was digging into the paper, making big ugly dark marks on the test page, then ripping through the paper. He stopped and tried to erase his markings, but the white paper smudged an ugly gray and ripped further.

The bell rang. Rowan sat and stared at his page, void of a single answer. Mr. G dismissed the class for recess one row at a time, collecting their tests as they filed out. He called Rowan's row last, and Rowan slowly made his way to the door, behind a group of fifth-grade girls eager to talk to Mr. G about their latest plan to write an article for the student paper. Mr. G smoothly ushered them out of the door as several boys called back into the classroom, "Hey, Rowan, hurry up. We have dibs on the playing field for some kick ball. Hurry, so we can pick teams!"

Mr. G blocked the boys from coming back in and told them, "Sorry fellas, you'll have to play without Rowan today. I have a special project and need him to help me this recess."

He closed the door and turned around to face the miserable Rowan. He reached for Rowan's test and looked at the torn and smeared page.

"You can retake this. Don't worry."

Rowan nodded, dreary-minded and disconnected.

"You want to talk about anything, or just take a break in here, Rowan?"

Rowan choked on the huge lump in his throat. Afraid he would cry some more, he just shook his head and gazed away from the steady eyes of his favorite teacher.

Mr. G nodded as if that was just fine. "That's cool, Rowan. Take your time. We're going to the library after recess. Do you want to hang out here or go with us?"

Rowan was still not able to speak, so Mr. G turned and walked back to his desk and started going through the papers, repeating, "Take your time, Rowan."

At that moment there was a pounding at the door and then a crash outside. Mr. G ignored it all, but then the wild knocking came again, so he walked over the door and opened it a crack.

Perry stood there. Apparently he had run into the ball box and toppled it over.

"What do you need, Perry? You know you should be out at recess."

"Uh, Mr. G. Uh, I just was wondering if Rowan was okay."

Mr. G looked at him a long time as Perry stood there twisting and wiggling, his hair falling uncontrolled over his forehead and his shirt buttoned wrong. But the boy's eyes were full of concern. It was the genuine Perry, thought Dale Grosnicholas.

"Listen, Perry. It's really good of you to check in on Rowan, but he's taking a break right now, helping me out. Everyone needs time and space sometimes. So just be cool and go have some recess. And, it would be very kind if you just kept your worry inside your head."

"Oh sure, Mr. G. But you know, sometimes I'm real sad too, and, uh, I thought maybe Rowan looked sad, and I've never seen Rowan sad before, even in kindergarten when I knocked down the best Lego project that he'd ever built. So you know, I just wondered, uh, you know, if he's okay."

"Perry, he's going to be okay. But, I'm proud of you for caring and I'm really proud of you for not blurting out in class today. I saw you show good self control. Way to go, buddy, way to go!"

Perry looked up at his teacher and a slow smile spread across his face as he realized he was being complimented.

"Well, sure, Mr. G. Well, I'll go back on the playground but tell Rowan I hope he feels better and I won't tell anyone, Mr. G. Honest. You can count on me!"

Olivia Howard was the third grade teacher at Paul Revere and also Rowan's maternal aunt. That noon, as Dale Grosnicholas slid into the chair next to her in the staff lounge and opened his sandwich bag, he made sure they were private, and then softly asked her, "Not to pry, but Rowan seems completely devastated this week. Do you know what's going on?"

Olivia sighed. She and the rest of the family had only had a few days themselves to absorb the shocking news: her sister, without any apparent emotion in her voice or face, told them that she and Warren were divorcing. That after fourteen years of what looked like the perfect marriage, it was over.

Olivia quietly shared the news with Mr. G. "My sister and brother-in-law are splitting. This all just happened."

"You don't have to tell me any details, Olivia, but I sure would like to help Rowan. He's an utter mess. Like I said, just devastated, and not able to talk about it. There's a thunder cloud over him."

"I can imagine, Dale. We're all stunned. We can't make any sense of it, and the worst is that Cecilia isn't talking, and Warren is simply gone. He's even going to move his business out of town. And none of us saw it coming! And we have no idea what happened, none of us, not even Mother or Papa. The boys must feel that their rug has been pulled out from under them. Mateo is close to my Papa, but Rowan is Daddy's little boy, always, so he has to be . . . destroyed."

She went on in a whisper as several other teachers came into the room. "I tried talking to Rowan this morning, and he wouldn't talk to me either. I hope our counselor can help him. He must be so angry." She turned and looked at the fifth grade teacher. "The kids admire you so much, Dale. You may be the best bet for helping him. I'm sorry. I'm not trying to dump it all on your shoulders. You're Rowan's teacher, not a therapist. But . . ." Olivia gulped hard and in a voice so quiet Dale had to lean in to hear, she added, ". . . I don't know what to do to help my nephews or my sister. I'm so sad. So sad."

Rowan somehow made it through the day, shielded by Mr. G. Across the room, Perry Schroeder was subdued, an unusual demeanor for this child. The boy seemed to ooze with empathy for his classmate, and this silenced him.

After school, Dale spent an hour with his chess club, and then took another hour preparing his lessons for the next day, which he did with headphones on, listening to his favorite jazz music. If he had not had the headphones on, he might have heard the intercom all-call for Rowan Schumacher. Around 5:00 he remembered he had planned to leave school early. His wife had invited some work colleagues to dinner and had asked him to make his famous chicken cordon bleu, which required hours of prep. He quickly stuffed the math tests into his bag to grade later that night.

Dale went straight to his car, not stopping at the office, and soon he was driving down the winding road that led from Paul Revere to the main county highway and on to his home in Amherst.

Dale almost missed seeing Rowan, but, out of the corner of his eye, he glimpsed a familiar red and green jacket through the trees in the woods. He immediately pulled over to the shoulder and had a quick thought as he ran towards where the jacket had disappeared into the trees: Julie will forgive me for being late, and this boy is walking through the worst time of his life. There was no question what he should do.

"Rowan!" he called out into the dense trees. "Rowan. It's Mr. G. Hang on. I'll join you."

It didn't take long for him to catch up with the boy who had slowed but not stopped in his pointless plunge through the trees and bushes.

"Hey, Rowan. Hold up. Let me catch my breath. Did you miss the bus?"

He checked his watch. "And the late activities bus, too?"

Rowan just stood there, facing the opposite direction, and was silent. His face was contorted and his cheeks were wet and flushed. Dale had never seen a more miserable child, and this was his most affable, easy-going fifth-grade jock.

"Which way are you headed? How about this direction? I think the bushes aren't so thick. Might be easier to walk this way."

"I don't care if it's easy. Doesn't matter to me if I get hurt or lost."

"I see. Hmm . . . Might matter to your mom, Rowan. And your dad."

"I don't care! They can go to hell!" The fifth grader was brazen in tone and language. But his lip trembled.

"My mom doesn't care about me. She doesn't care about anyone else! She only cares about her own stupid self. I hate her!"

This outburst floated out into the woods. Dale didn't comment immediately, just walked beside and then behind Rowan as the passageway through the pines grew narrow.

"You feel a lot of anger now. I understand that. And you know, I think most people would understand that. In fact . . ." Dale took a look at the boy's face before continuing, ". . . I would even imagine that your mom and dad understand how angry you are and wouldn't hold that against you, Rowan."

"Yeah, sure! Mr. G, my mom kicked my dad out of the house and he's gone, and I don't know when I can see him again, and anyway she says he won't be moving back home, ever again. Ever!"

The boy sank to his knees in the middle of the trees and sobbed. Dale squatted about three feet away but made no attempt to touch the boy; he just let Rowan wail for awhile until his tears subsided and his hiccups became further apart. Rowan looked as if he could go to sleep right there and then, he was so tired. Dale was not a father, but he ached for the boy nonetheless. He stayed with him in silence for some time as the quiet of the woods absorbed the pain of the boy.

Finally Dale spoke again, not looking at Rowan but sitting down on the dirt next to him and gazing into the trees.

"Rowan, when I was twelve, my parents divorced. I wasn't really surprised because they were always fighting, loud awful fights, so when my dad left, it was better in some ways because there wasn't so much fighting, but there was a lot of sadness for my mom, for my sister and me, too. Everything felt all topsy-turvy, like my world had been turned upside down. And it was extra bad because I didn't have any friends whose parents had divorced, so I felt like my family and I were freaks. I'm guessing that's what it feels like for you right now, and Mateo too. And probably even more so if you had no idea that things weren't okay with your parents. You were really caught by surprise."

He paused for a moment, and Rowan looked at him briefly, then nodded.

"Rowan, for me it took a long time to realize that it wasn't my dad's fault and it wasn't my mom's fault, and it especially wasn't my fault. It was just the way things were. They were really unhappy but they didn't set out to make my life rotten. It just happened. It took me a long time, until I was an adult in fact, to figure that out, so no one expects you to figure it out today or next week, or even next year, Rowan. You have a lot of feelings inside you and that means you're normal. I guess that's what I want you to know right now. You're okay and it's normal to feel the way you do."

Mr. G could sense the boy listening to him although he didn't say a word.

"The other thing I want you to consider is this, Rowan. Your mom loves you." When the boy snorted in protest, he continued. "No, Rowan, I don't expect you to feel that right now, but I'm going to bet my whole farm - why, I would wager my car and my saxophone both - on the fact that your mom loves you and that if she knows you are not home right now, she's probably worried sick about you."

Rowan didn't protest but he looked down at the dirt and pushed a stick into the dirt over and over, digging a hole deeper and deeper.

"Remember, Rowan, something went wrong between your mom and your dad. Something other people can't begin to understand, and that's really frustrating for you, I know. But grownups are weird sometimes, Rowan. Maybe I should say that life gets weird for grownups sometimes. And sometimes it's a lot better to be a kid, even though you feel like you don't have any control."

Rowan stopped digging and sat there silent, wasted and tired, and perhaps open to what his teacher was saying.

"So there are two things I want you to remember for tonight, try to hang on to this. One, it's okay to feel the way you feel. And two, your parents love you despite how selfish they appear to you right now."

"Mr. G What if you're not right about that?"

"Hmm. Then I'll buy you a banana split at Shakey's."

The boy almost smiled. Almost.

"Hey, I'm getting cold sitting out here. Feels like it's going to drop below freezing tonight. Maybe we'll get that spring snow and be able to build ice caves on our outdoor education week!"

The teacher and student got up and began making their way out of the woods and towards the road.

"Can I give you a lift back to Pine Junction?"

"Yeah. I gotta go home. I got homework to do."

The boy slipped into the 1968 Mustang, Mr. G's second favorite possession after his jazz saxophone. A tiny part of Rowan was still capable of being thrilled to be riding in Mr. G's car.

"Mr. G? I hate my mom."

"I understand that, Rowan. But remember she's probably as miserable as you are in her own adult sort of way. Hang on to that thought if you can. Meanwhile you have a math test tomorrow to retake, and the guys are needing you to win their baseball game. And, by the way, Rowan, would you be willing to partner with Perry on the geography project? He really knows his stuff but has trouble getting it down and organized on a chart. You seem to have a good way of helping him out."

Rowan nodded.

As they turned onto the road leading to Pine Junction, a familiar old Volvo station wagon sat at the stop sign ready to turn towards the school. It was Rowan's mom, Cecilia. Dale pulled his car over and parked on the shoulder of the road. Cecilia jumped out of the car and ran over. Slowly Rowan opened his door and stood there.

Cecilia grabbed her youngest son and rocked him back and forth in a hug that at first Rowan received with stiffness, awkward and defensive, not wanting to respond in kind, especially not with his teacher standing there. But finally he caved, and the hurt little boy inside the angry fifth-grader dissolved, despite the presence of Mr. G.

And as the white-faced Cecilia murmured, "Rowan, I was so worried. I love you so much. I was so scared that I'd lost you," Dale Grosnicholas drove off to explain the evening's menu to his wife.

They would have a different dinner tonight, perhaps chicken picatta. For Dale it would be flavored with memories and bittersweet thoughts about human relationships. And that was just his own life. He sighed as he thought of the long, road ahead for Rowan and his family. Nothing would be easy for any of them for a long time to come. But from his own experience Dale knew that time and work and passions could heal many wounds. Would Rowan find the magic combination and would he find the people he needed to help him reach the other side of his pain? How much time would the boy need? Dale resolved right then to keep an eye on the boy as long as he could.

5

DREAM WORK

Vic & Cecilia

1978 - 2001

The choir sang its last "Amen," and the mood changed from musically reverent to verbally casual. Choir rehearsal was over. Men and women, as well as a few teenagers, handed their choir binders to Cecilia, picked up their coats, and made their way out the door. Those with young children at home or their own homework yet to do made hasty exits, and those with more time on their hands leisurely chatted before heading out into the cold New England winter.

Conversational tidbits drifted back into the warm choir room.

"Don't forget book club at my house this Friday - I hope everyone actually reads the book this time."

"Good luck at your doctor's appointment tomorrow, Henry."

"Say Dan, did you see that new Jack Lemmon movie?"

Some gossip slipped in: "I heard the Sullivans won't be attending their own son's wedding. Can you imagine?"

And a few irreverent comments about the weather, too: "Colder than a witch's tit out here."

Car doors slammed and soon the room was empty except for Cecilia fulfilling one of her duties as choir secretary, checking through the choir binders, making sure each song was included and in correct sequence, and slipping in an order of worship for Sunday's service, plus a note on choir business. She did have a baby boy at home, but he was recently weaned and being cared for this evening by his doting grandfather, so she could take her time getting things in order in the comfortable choir room located just off the church chancel.

First Congregational Church of Pine Junction, Massachusetts, had a long tradition of good music, and, along with the premiere organ for miles around, it also had a well-established choir. Choir had been a big part of Cecilia's growing up, and she moved right back into it when she returned a year ago to her home town with a new husband and, soon afterward, a new baby. As the new librarian at the public library, it was natural for Cecilia to help the director organize the church's music library. In charge of that music program, doubling as the church organist and choir director, Vic Dalloway himself had only been with the Pine Junction church for less than two years.

Cecilia looked up and smiled at Vic, who had come back into the room and was straightening some chairs. She said casually, "Oh, Vic, you were in my dream last night!"

She looked down again at her work, or she would have seen the instant reddening spread over Vic's face. He didn't know what to say, but managed to choke out some sort of neutral response which was not very welcoming to further conversation; what came out of his mouth was the exact opposite of what he was feeling.

Vic's presence in this little town was due to the fine organ donated by none other than Cecilia's maternal grandparents, whose endowment had also supported an organist to match the caliber of the lovely Casavant that was central to the church.

He had only been in Pine Junction for three months when Cecilia moved back to her home town and, in a flurry, introduced her attorney husband to her old acquaintances, bought an old house with a picket fence and, early in 1977, gave birth to a healthy little boy who had his mother's dark hair and eyes.

Cecilia was pleasant to everyone but not truly close to anyone, and the first attribute was so strong that no one really noticed that she kept her own counsel much of the time. She loved singing and music in general, and in a small town, the local church choir was an obvious outlet for her.

Vic had fallen for this dark-haired soprano with every fiber of his spare frame including his virgin body and aesthetic spirit. It had been a pure agony to be around her, and yet he would have died if she had not been there. This uneasy alliance of pain and joy was new to him. He had all sorts of dreams, both waking fantasies and sleeping dreams, dominated by Cecilia's deep dark eyes and hair, engaging smile, and lush body. Vic was an honorable man, a shy and inexperienced man, as well as one who knew who buttered his employment toast, and so he clamped down on his emotions in a manner that would have made his ancestors proud.

But he suffered. He suffered like a man of a different time and place, not at all like a man of a modern permissive culture.

Seeing Warren Schumacher every Sunday in church added to the pain he felt. He had nothing against Warren, but Cecilia's husband represented a position Vic so envied that Vic found himself avoiding the man if at all possible. Warren, being himself rather aloof, didn't give Vic much notice once he stood up from his organ bench. Warren appreciated good music and so held Dalloway in high regard for his talent, but nothing else connected him to the man.

Cecilia's little boy, Mateo, now a year old and full of smiles and good nature, became the object of Vic's affection, in his own dry manner. He certainly didn't smother the boy, but he did pay attention to him. It was one way he could openly admire a part of Cecilia that was safe and accepted by everyone in town.

Months had gone by like this. Vic didn't see the possibility of anything changing, and he was not sure how he could go on living in such a state of animated agitation. But somehow he did, day after day, and he managed to keep his love hidden from everyone, from Cecilia and even from all the observant choir members. The minister himself, Carl Prescott, was an astute theologian and progressive minister, but hardly one for observing human behavior. Living within his own Prescott bubble, he never noticed his new organist's robust but secret infatuation with the married daughter of one of the town's most esteemed families.

All Vic had to do was be his own eccentric self: sardonic, focused upon music above all else, and soon, very soon, all those who lived in his world came to see him as a caricature of himself. He found very quickly that this persona became a safe place to hide his burning passion for young Mrs. Schumacher.

This was how Vic was existing on this night after choir practice when Cecilia's friendly voice told him that he had been in her dream. She didn't notice that Vic had not asked her to tell him more. She was used to his abrupt ways, and they did not offend her at all. She admired his musicianship and was oblivious that he might harbor romantic interest in anyone, much less herself, so she was very comfortable talking to him and explaining her dream.

"Oh, you know, not a big, bad dream," she volunteered. "No blood or violence. Wasn't frightened, didn't wake up shaking."

She picked up the next binder and stopped for a moment as she reviewed her dream.

"It was just one of those frustrating dreams. Ever have those?"

Cecilia didn't notice Vic's lack of response. "I have this recurring dream, Vic. Drives me crazy. Why, oh why, do we have recurring dreams?"

She laughed and talked on, less to Vic than to herself.

"I don't have a clue what my dreams mean, especially this one. It's all about telephones. Can you believe it? Telephones. How boring."

She brushed her hair back from her brow, in a movement that caused Vic's stomach to clutch.

"Telephones! In every dream I'm supposed to do something important, something urgent, and so I pick up my phone and try to dial and, every time, I screw up and cannot complete the call. I try again, and again and again. I never can make that call!"

She put aside the last binder and put the stack into the wooden box where they were stored between rehearsals and services.

"You know what else is funny, Vic?"

Cecilia came over to Vic, coat over her arm and bag on her shoulder, but she was clearly still thinking about her dreams. Her very closeness made Vic's heart beat like a hammer in his chest. He was afraid she would actually notice his shirt moving like in a cartoon, and therefore he missed his cue to answer her question. She acted as though he had responded.

"What's so funny is that I've had these dreams for years, and they have changed only in the style of the phone. I used to dream about the old dial phone, remember those? I would almost get the number dialed when my finger would slip and the dial would slide back with the wrong number, so I would have to start all over again, over and over."

She dropped her bag to the floor and started to put her arm in her coat sleeve, still talking.

"And then we got pushbutton phones and my dreams just morphed along into frustrating attempts to punch the right number. I would get to the last number and then, darn it, hit the wrong button! Oh, so very frustrating! And, sometimes I would drop the phone or lose the phone, or my eyes would blur and I would not be able to see the number I was supposed to be punching."

Vic stood there not realizing he could have helped her with her coat, a perfectly socially acceptable bit of good manners, not breaking any code of conduct, so she struggled into her coat sleeve over her thick sweater.

"And the other night, in my dream I was standing in a pay phone booth, a red one like in London, but I was here in Pine Junction! The operator kept asking me for money, I was hearing the pips, but I couldn't count out the right amount of coins, couldn't figure out the English money, so I couldn't make my call!"

Cecilia laughed at her own story-telling and Vic cracked a feeble smile, hoping she would never stop talking and never stop laughing and never go home, and yet wishing she would go away so he could jump into his own metaphorical cold shower.

She finally got her coat on, and touching Vic's arm affectionately, she told him good night and headed out the door. As she was pushing the door open she turned and laughed again.

"Maybe someday there'll be phones you can just carry with you, small enough for your pocket or purse, and you can make calls wherever you may be! Do you think that's possible? Like space age technology! I wonder if my phone dreams will keep up with technology? I guess I'll have to keep these stupid dreams going and find out."

Cecilia stepped out into the frigid night and was gone. It was completely quiet in the church. Vic was the only one left, as usual. Reverend Prescott was home in his parsonage, by his fire, meal tucked into his stout belly, book in front of him, a contented man with a big intellect, satisfied mind, superficial emotions, and a long life behind him. At the church, standing in the middle of his choir room, was the opposite kind of man, a gifted man in turmoil, confused, with deep but unexpressed emotions, a young life suspended.

Only hours later did Vic remember that Cecilia had never told him where he had fit into her dream.

Vic Dalloway was obviously not a teenager anymore. But even when he had been a teen in Canada, there had been no luxury of teenage sexual fantasies experienced, and then explored and graphically discussed with friends. His teen years had passed in a blur of unhappiness as an only child in avoidance of his father's wrath and his mother's passive fading from life. Music was always Vic's escape, his therapy, his salvation. Fortunately he showed great talent early. It was the one aspect of his life in which he was sure and strong. He would have sacrificed everything to keep making music. And he did sacrifice his father's respect, earned his father's anger. He also alienated himself from potential friends. He was too myopic to see that had he broadened his musical repertoire, he could have played piano and organ in a rock band as well as in the great cathedrals and concert halls. What a different life it would have been. But he spent far too much energy during his teenage and university years trying to match his father anger for anger. It was the only way he could see to survive. He was no match for his father, though. Vic Dalloway was at heart a gentle and loving soul, much more like his remote mother. But he had enough of his father's stubbornness, as well as well-honed musical talent, to succeed in the classical music field in his home province, and then throw it in his father's face, pay off his financial debt to his father, and leave Manitoba and even Canada, too. He abandoned his parents for a new life in the States. Or, you could say he left the toxicity of his family home and made a brand new start as a new man in a new country.

In the end, it was music that carried him along and music that sheltered him from emotional entanglements. He lived simply and with one mind until he met Cecilia. The house of cards he had carefully built as his fortress came crashing down the minute she put out her hand to introduce herself and he looked in her eyes.

Vic was over twenty-five when he met Cecilia, but socially and sexually he was a child. He recognized this fact in the five seconds he held Cecilia's handshake in his. He forgot to let go, and she laughed and withdrew her hand.

This retarded state of being became his shame, and in time it became the shield that protected him from his own passions and the opinion of the world.

He also never stopped anyone from assuming he was gay. A gay man, not out of the closet, was a person his progressive community could understand in the 1970's. He was, after all, a musician. And that was it. He brought them to tears with his musical talent, and that was all they really needed to know about Vic Dalloway. He had his role. He lived into his role until it protected his soul.

In the years that followed, the role Vic played kept him in Cecilia's presence, but his choices tormented him. One solution, as he saw it, was to leave Pine Junction forever and try to forget her, but that thought left him feeling agonizingly empty. The idea of trying to seduce her, she a married woman with first one son and three years later a second little boy, was a thought he saved only for his fantasies. He never would have crossed that line. It was not in him, and he wondered why. Was it because he didn't have the nerve? Or was it because he was simply too honorable to have an affair with a married woman? Did he love her so much that he would never have put Cecilia into such a compromising position? Or was it that he could not imagine that she might regard him with anything but friendship, or that she would regard him any differently than the rest of the community did, as a stereotype, an eccentric, a young man who was also old, and perhaps genderless as well. He felt that everyone saw his artistic talent, but nothing more.

As the years went by, Vic did come to believe that Cecilia regarded him as a friend. He was so moved by this that he settled for it, and regarded her friendship as more than settling, as the highest honor he could ever be worthy of receiving. He dared not dream of more. That wasn't true. He did dream of more, but he kept a careful check on those dreams.

So what does a healthy man in his thirties do with his unrequited sexual drives? Vic gave it a shot now and then. He went out of town, far enough away where he could be anonymous. He went to bars and clubs. He was not good at flirting but his needs were obvious and there was usually someone to engage. He had some sexual experiences, none of which were good, and some which were downright humiliating.

The women's responses were rarely kind.

"What is the matter with you? What kind of man are you?"

But, periodically he continued to try to have an experience to help him, at least temporarily, forget Cecilia's face.

And not just her face. He wanted to be wrapped in her body. He had watched her nurse one baby, discreetly but not completely, and then get pregnant and birth, nurse, and wean another little boy. Vic could not express how much this moved him. It drove him crazy, but it was so much more than pure sexual desire. Cecilia was perfection as a mother and a woman. The classical music engulfing his days and the classical art work he absorbed at the Metropolitan, gave him that same sense of lust as well, all mixed in with spiritual longings, and Cecilia was his Madonna as well as his earthly desire.

Vic wondered if he would spend the rest of his life in this state of suppressed agitation, this suspension. Then, one night he got some help from a surprising source. A pick-up from a bar. It was a seedy bar in the college town of Amherst. Vic was half-heartedly attempting again to free himself of his exploding yearnings, drinking a bit more than he usually allowed himself, especially when so relatively close to Pine Junction.

The young woman who invited him to go back to her apartment didn't look any different than the others; each time he hoped it might somehow ease his tension if not free his soul. But she was wiser than most, or perhaps just more compassionate. After Vic's clumsy attempts at love making, she guided him to at least some success in releasing his pressing need. But what followed was different than his past encounters. No criticism, well-earned as it might be. No anger at being used, although it was apparent.

This young woman sat up next to Vic in bed, pulled out a cigarette, offered one to Vic, which he took. Vic lay there in misery, ready to slip out of the room. But, before he could collect himself and his clothes, she stopped him with this comment: "You know, you're supposed to look happy after sex. You look like you want to kill yourself. Are you cheating on someone? Feeling guilty or something? I don't think I'm that bad, am I?" Her laugh was relaxed; she was quite confident of herself.

"Oh, no, no. No, not at all. And . . . uh, thank you."

"So you must be cheating on your wife or girlfriend." All this said calmly, with no judgment, like a psychologist in a therapy session.

"No, of course not. That's not it!" Vic was indignant and yet it hit him that he did feel he was cheating on Cecilia, as irrational as that might be.

"Ah, damn it, guy, you really are unhappy. Want to tell me about it? I don't have class until 9:00 tomorrow, so start talking if you like."

Vic stared at this young woman, a stranger, who lay on the bed next to him, naked as he was. She was not ashamed of her body or of her desires. She was shameless and yet so accepting. Something moved in Vic and to his amazement he lay there not noticing his own nakedness or her lovely body either, and told this young woman about his love for the unattainable Cecilia.

It was, he thought later, like a confessional. Vulnerable and stripped of all pride, he gave confession to this naked priestess lying on her crumpled sheets, while she smoked and listened, kindly but also with detachment. It felt safe to Vic.

After Vic finished explaining his tortured passion, his listener didn't seem appalled.

"You say it's been five years since you met her?"

"Yes, five years."

She snubbed her cigarette out in a saucer beside the bed and turned towards him..

"You know what? This's a love story that you just don't hear any more. It's weird but beautiful. You're one for the ages, you and this torch you're carrying. It'd be an honor to have someone feel that way about me. Well, in fact, for me it would be a pain in the ass, but I love the whole romantic image."

Vic didn't say anything, just continued to stare unhappily up at the ancient leak stain on the ceiling.

"So, it seems to me that you're never going to make a pass at her or you would've already done so. And you don't want to move far away. And you think her marriage is not about ready to dissolve so you can just wait in the wings to grab her, right?" She paused as she thought more. "Most women usually have some idea when they are being worshipped from afar."

She saw Vic's head shake at this.

"Okay, so she's not aware at all. Hmm. Well, you don't seem to get much happiness from fucking, so could you be any more miserable if you got serious about being celibate? You know, really did it right, spiritually and all? I gotta say, it's not for me, but there're all sorts of ways to live. Straight or gay, active or not active. You're a church guy, you said, so just go a little more religious and find out how those monks do it."

She laughed and jumped out of bed.

"Hey, I'm starving. I have some peanut butter and crackers, and a beer or two, that's about all. You want some?"

Vic declined, got dressed, and with more dignity than he usually mustered after these sorts of nights, he thanked her. He felt that there was more he should do, so he held out his hand. She laughed out loud, and grabbed him in a big hug, still naked and still so young.

"Good luck, my friend. Hope you figure it all out. Life's too short to be so unhappy. Go figure out what will make you the happiest - to pine away in mystical love, or to get on with things. For you, I think you might be happiest to worship from afar. And you know what, why not? Takes all kinds to make the world go around. You're a good guy, I can tell."

That very night, Vic Dalloway decided to take a vow of celibacy. He saw no plausible alternative that was more desirable. His love for Cecilia was pure and to his mind, perfect. As the years unfolded their friendship progressed, but the boundaries were never crossed. It was like an old-fashioned platonic relationship and Vic cherished it. His decision was almost satisfying to him. If he could not have Cecilia as his own, he would not have anyone else. He would rather live with the ache of not having her than to seek a life without her presence. The love he held for her became a comfort zone to him while it also fueled his artistic edge. And it became such a part of him that when Cecilia and Warren split up fourteen years after the birth of their first son, with no warning to the community around them, Vic was unable to disrupt the status quo and pursue more. Cecilia, now also single, and Vic, perpetually unattached, continued to have a chaste kinship that grew stronger with the years.

It seemed to Vic that it would always remain thus, and by 1992 - the night Cecilia told him of her phone dreams - he was at peace with it.

One day, Vic and Cecilia were sitting in the church parlor going through old musical scores, trying to decide what to sing for the 2001 Lent season. The phone rang in the new pastor's office and through the walls they could hear Reverend Rex Randall, Dr. Prescott's replacement, answer with his enthusiastic voice.

Cecilia suddenly laughed out loud and put down the musical score.

"That phone ringing reminds me, Vic. I had one of my crazy dreams last night. Have I ever told you about my recurring dream? About the phones? I was out by a lake somewhere, not sure where, and I needed to make a phone call. Needed help for something, not sure what it was about. And every time I tried to touch the right numbers on my cell phone, I'd get the wrong number. I had to keep deleting and starting again. It felt like my hands were wearing thick gloves and I couldn't get the right numbers. Oh gosh, Vic, it was so frustrating."

She picked up the musical score again and looked at it. "Looks like we marked that we sang this one in 1987. Such a long time ago But time goes fast." She looked up at Vic, still thinking of her dream, and asked him lightly: "Have you ever been so frustrated you wanted to just scream, Vic?"

6

LEAVING HOME

Mateo

1995

From his second-story classroom, Mateo could gaze out the window across the treetops to the hills beyond. All his senior year he had sat in this desk, looking out that window, over and beyond to where he could feel the beat of the City beckoning to him. He completed his math work, passed his tests, did his homework, but increasingly, as the year progressed, he answered fewer and fewer questions, participated in class discussion less and less. Math came easily to him, and he maintained his grades at a high level, but his teacher, Jillian Jonsdotter, watched him slip away from his classmates and his town, day by day, more and more. Wanting to respect Mateo's privacy she hesitated to mention anything to her colleague at the Consolidated High School, the warm and gracious Pedro Sanchez, Mateo's grandfather. And on this subject, Jillian, as a young teacher, didn't have the nerve to approach Mateo's intimidating grandmother, veteran English teacher, Victoria Sanchez. But Jillian continue to watch the lean young man in the third row, left aisle, next to the window.

She watched him until she couldn't stand it anymore.

"Mateo, may I see you after class today?" she quietly spoke to him when he entered the next day.

"Sure." He nodded but didn't reflect any concern. He had nothing to feel guilty about, nothing that should have elicited any negative teacher or administrative attention, and in fact had forgotten his teacher's request by the time he slipped into his seat, opened his math book and notes, and then, as had become his habit, turned his head to the window.

Jillian restrained herself from pulling down the blinds. Some teachers taught with the windows covered to reduce distraction, but in her short three years of teaching, she prided herself in being able to keep her students tuned in to her, even the math-phobic students.

"Mateo, your mind seems a million miles away these days."

Mateo looked up from his backpack, intent on putting his books away after class. Jillian stood near his desk as the other students poured out of the room and into the hall.

Mateo smiled his easy smile. But he looked out the window and away from his teacher's eyes. "Oh, I suppose I have senioritis, Ms. Jonsdotter."

"Hm. I suppose I should be glad you are holding your own in class, Mateo, but I don't see you working with any enthusiasm. Not up to your potential."

At this last phrase, Mateo's face darkened. He rarely showed any emotion other than an easy-going openness, and Jillian was taken aback.

"You know, Ms. Jonsdotter. No disrespect, but I'm getting pretty tired of hearing that phrase. 'My potential.' What is that supposed to mean? It seems like everyone else has some plan for my life and you know . . . ." He didn't complete his thought but instead turned his whole body and looked out the window again. He towered over his teacher but she did not feel threatened, although clearly he was angry, a rare sight. Speaking through tense jaw and gritted teeth, he added more explanation.

"I don't see myself following anyone else's path. Just because I'm a good student, or because my classmates are hell-bent on an Ivy League school, or even because everyone else in my family went to university, doesn't mean I have to, or that I want to."

"You have a good brain for math, Mateo, as well as so many other subjects. You speak Spanish fluently, and you have mastered French as well. You are very well-read and apparently you can ace any class from World Literature to Chemistry. Your SAT scores were great. You were admitted to many colleges, I hear. Did you accept one of them yet?"

"No."

"Any favorites?"

"No." Mateo looked down at his foot for a moment and seemed fascinated with turning the heel of his Adidas back and forth. Then he looked straight down into the serious face of his teacher. Her look was earnest. Although only twenty-six years old herself, she seemed worlds older than her students because of her intense involvement in her subject and her teaching mission. He respected her, but he could see that she had a different passion than that which burned in his soul these days.

"Ms. Jonsdotter, I don't dislike school. And I've enjoyed learning all my life. Heck, you have to know that, growing up with my mother the librarian, my dad the attorney, and my grandparents, the consummate teachers, plus all the other educators in my family, I've lived and breathed learning about everything all my life. And you're right, I read all the time, I read everything, every genre, every subject. But there's only one thing I really want to do, and that is play music and hear music."

"Did you apply to any music schools, Mateo? Math and music are often seen as excellent partners."

Mateo ran his hand through his dark hair and burst out with some exasperation. "No, No! I don't want to study anything. I want to just live it, feel it, play it, listen to it. I just want to be." And here he pulled his backpack onto his shoulder and, again staring out the window, his eyes got a far-off look. "I just want to be free."

"I see." She didn't. Her experience had been so different.

"Yeah, well. I doubt it. Most people don't get it. But that's what I want."

He moved on away down the aisle, but his good manners reappeared, and he apologized. "I'm sorry, I have to get to next period. I have a report to present in Government. I don't think I'm behind in any math assignments, right? And I'll be completing my course work early. I plan on graduating early. I have the units. But don't tell anyone, please."

He looked at her as if sorry he had spilled his secret, the secret that had been brewing inside him all the hours he had gazed out the window over the school year. "Please. Especially don't tell my grandpa. I want to talk to him myself."

Jillian looked at him. Such an attractive young man, and yet his pleading with her brought out a vulnerability in him that she had never noticed. Mateo was effortlessly popular with students of both sexes. The boys appreciated his easy-going spirit, musical ability, and athleticism that always lent a healthy fun to any P.E. or pickup game. Beyond spirited play, he was not competitive in any setting and smiled his way through the pleadings of the coaches to join up with this team or that. He loved good class discussion, at least until recently. While very knowledgeable, he never lorded his intellectual prowess. As for the girls, many were in love with him, but he didn't attach himself to any one girl as far as his teacher had observed in her three years at the high school. A charming, yet sincere kid, Jillian thought to herself. And, she thought with sadness, so bright. Such a good math student. Harvard. Or her alma mater, Princeton. No question. The world could be his oyster.

He was still looking at her, with a question on his face. She walked back to her desk to get ready for her next class, and reassured him. "Mateo, I won't mention your plans to anyone. But I'll be hoping you reconsider."

"Not even the guidance counselor? Please."

She nodded. "But talk to your grandparents and your parents soon. Okay?"

He nodded, and slipped out the door.

Mateo was an enigma to others, but a very simple guy to his own mind.

The night before Mateo left home, he had gone to bed early, as if urging the morning to come more quickly. He didn't have a Class of 1995 farewell party with friends the night before. There were no long lingering goodbye kisses from an adoring girlfriend, although there were several girls who would have gladly volunteered. Despite his good intentions, Mateo had not been able to sleep all night in his excitement. But he was up early and dressed, a large duffel bag full of clothes and books and a jacket all staged by the front door, with his ever-present guitar case leaning next to it.

The day Mateo left home, the skies promised a rain shower in Pine Junction before noon, but the morning was fresh and expectant. He stopped in the kitchen to have breakfast with his mom. Cecelia Sanchez Schumacher had not been able to sleep either, but it was not for excitement. She came to the kitchen in her nightgown, dark hair messy from the night spent in motion on her pillow. Mateo didn't notice her swollen eyes because Cecilia put on a cheerful countenance as she saw her son all ready to leave.

"A good breakfast to see you off, Mateo?"

"Ah, well, Mom, thanks, but you know I want to stop and see Grand Pedro before he heads to school, so I don't really have time for much."

"Mateo, I insist. Eat it for me if not for your own health. Papa won't leave for work for an hour at least, so you have time. Let's see eggs, pancakes, maybe waffles, or bacon?"

"Mom, really, no, not all that. It'd make my stomach hurt."

Cecilia looked at him sharply. "Stomach upset?"

"Nah, just excited, Mom. This's a big day for me, and I'm too hepped up to eat much. How about some toast and some of Grandma's orange marmalade? That'd be great."

Mateo wanted to get going, but he was also nothing if not a diplomat and realized he should be accommodating to his mother.

Cecilia was not born yesterday either, and she inwardly rolled her eyes at her son's display of tolerance for her desire for a few more minutes of time together. She kept reminding herself that, of course, Mateo didn't know the degree of her heartache. In fact, he had no idea at all about her sorrow at this emptying of her nest. It was bad enough that Rowan, her fifteen-year-old, had convinced his father to pay for a private boarding school, and so she had lost him from her home a year ago, but now Mateo was leaving too. And, he was so happy to be going that he didn't notice how painful this was for her.

Mateo had been good company in the four years since she and Warren had split up. He had sat with Cecilia in the evenings sometimes and played Scrabble or Cribbage, or played the guitar while she sat in her big chair and read. And when she sat down at the baby grand in the corner of her living room and played away the hours, he often sat nearby engrossed in his own book, or, even on those most rare and exquisite moments, he would pull out his guitar and play along with her. But somehow Cecilia always sensed that Mateo's heart and mind were elsewhere, while his body impatiently waited to reach an age when he could leave home. Mateo had never been hers, not really. She had birthed him, and raised him, and loved him with all her heart, but he belonged to himself and to himself only, not even to his soul mate all these past eighteen years, his grandfather. He was his own man, not a boy anymore, and she knew she could only wish him well and pray he would be safe and happy.

But this ache could not be soothed by any of her usual cures of books, work, music, or garden. This hurt she would have to carry along with her and give it due respect, because this loss was not lightening as she tried to get used to the idea. She knew her father would carry the same pain, but Cecilia and Pedro could never verbalize their feelings. Too many secrets in each of their own lives had complicated their conversations, no matter how deeply they loved each other.

Cecelia cut a slice of bread and toasted it, got the marmalade from the refrigerator, poured Mateo some orange juice, and started to make him some coffee, when Mateo intervened.

"Hey, let me do the coffee, Mom."

"You don't like my coffee, do you?" Cecilia softened her comment with a smile and a squeeze of Mateo's shoulder as he stood next to her at the counter.

"I learned some better ways to make it when I visited Amherst the other day, and it was the best cup of coffee I ever had. I think I might look for a job at a coffee shop when I get to New York."

Cecilia looked at Mateo's tall frame, dark hair like her own, starting to grow longer as he was leaving high school behind for good now. He was exceptionally good-looking. This worried her some. Would he be safe? Would he be taken advantage of? She dismissed that thought, knowing her son. Another opposite thought crossed after that. Would life be too easy for him? Even in the big city where competition was fierce, would life unfold with little effort on his part and flow too smoothly? Not that she wanted hardships for her boy, but one did grow by making mistakes and dealing with adversity. As she reflected more, aware of Mateo's coffee-making beside her, she considered that life had come easily for Mateo.

Then she jolted. How could she forget her divorce, how shocked the community and her family had been by the Schumachers' split? Rowan had been so angry she could read it in his whole being. Mateo had seemed to take it in stride and go on with his life, growing even closer to his grandfather, playing his guitar endlessly. He had not been rude or argumentative with her, and he had been polite with his father. He sailed on with his life. Or, so it had seemed. Cecilia had not been able to penetrate this exterior, and since Mateo's demeanor had been easier to live with than Rowan's glowering anger, she had wanted to accept that Mateo was fine with the state of his home life these last four years.

Of course she had known all along that Mateo was altered forever by his parents' divorce, but she had been too cowardly to bring it out in the open.

Now Mateo cheerfully handed his mom a cup of coffee as a joke before pulling it back. She was a tea drinker and disliked coffee. Both of them smiled at this old scenario he had played out ever since he started drinking coffee himself. He sat down at the table and took a sip from the cup.

"Ah, that's a much better cup of coffee."

"Mateo, are you sure I can't give you a ride? I can take the day off work and drive you in to Peter's apartment."

Mateo stifled a shudder at the thought of making his grand departure, his escape, to his new life by being dropped off by his mother.

"Oh, no, Mom, I have it all figured out. I'll pick up the county bus at the junction, take that to the train station, and catch the commuter train down to the City."

As a concession to his mother, he added, "And don't worry. I'll stay with Peter Rushford for a week while I figure out a place to live and find a job. I won't starve and I won't live on the street. I promise you. And I will be careful about who I meet and where I go."

He stood up, wiped the crumbs off his mouth, swallowed his last sip of coffee standing up, and walked to the door.

"Don't forget to go to the bathroom, Mateo. It will be a long time before you get to a clean bathroom." Cecilia could hear how pathetic she sounded, and Mateo's withering glance confirmed this.

"Mom!"

"Sorry, dear. I have a different kind of excitement than you today, so I guess I am being over-protective. I apologize."

Mateo came over and gave his mom an exuberant hug, lifting her feet off the floor. "Hey, Mom, be excited for me, okay? I'm off to a new life!"

She nodded and held him tight for as long as she thought he would tolerate.

She looked up into his restless face, bent his head down to her and kissed his forehead, then let him go. Really let him go.

"I love you, Mateo. Take care of yourself."

"Will do, Mom," he tossed over his shoulder as he bounded down the old wooden front stairs.

Cecilia focused on those stairs for a moment realizing that they had not borne up well to the last winter's heavy snowfall. Thinking of this, she almost forgot to watch Mateo disappear down the street to stop at her parents' home to say goodbye to his grandfather.

Pedro was waiting for Mateo. He was dressed in his usual teaching outfit of corduroy sports jacket and pants. He always wore a tie, no matter how clothing styles changed for teachers. He had been teaching a very long time and had his standards for dress firmly in place. He smiled welcomingly when Mateo swung up the path to the front door, and he walked out to greet the young man. At eighteen Mateo resembled Pedro's own youthful image in the one photograph taken of him at that age, as a young army private heading off to war. He said a quick prayer of thanks that Mateo was not off to such a future, at least not on this particular spring morning.

"Grand Pedro. I'm off! This's the day!"

"You look like you're ready."

"I am."

The two looked at each other during a quiet but comfortable pause. They had been best of friends since Mateo's birth. Memories flashed through Pedro's mind, standing there on the porch, but Mateo was not looking back at all. He carried the memories of his time with his grandfather deep in his fabric and had no need to analyze them. He simply felt happy to be with his grandfather, always. It was the complete acceptance he received from the older man, that freed Mateo to be himself. This was the gift he had received every day of his life from Pedro. That, and his grandfather's infectious love of music. But Mateo was not thinking of any of this. He was only thinking of the future.

If anyone could have stopped Mateo from leaving home, stopped him from pursuing the crazy dream of freedom that burned within him, steered him towards university, it would have been Pedro. The boy and his grandfather had been inseparable since his birth, and there was no greater influence on the young man than his mysterious and intelligent grandfather. But at this juncture, Pedro understood the inevitability of Mateo's flight, and he simply put out his arms and embraced the young man to send him on his way. As he did so, he slipped an envelope into Mateo's pocket, patted it and said, "Open this when you get to your destination today. Help you out until you get that first pay check."

"Thanks. Bye, Grand Pedro. I'll write. Or call."

Pedro nodded, but wondered about the likelihood.

As Mateo jumped down the porch steps two at a time, guitar case and duffle bag bouncing on either side of him, he called back, "I'll send you an address so when I get my CD player, you can send me those CDs, okay?"

And finally as he reached the gate, he called back, "Oh, tell Grandma goodbye from me."

And then he was gone down the street. Pedro turned around and saw his wife, Victoria, looking out from behind the curtains, her face unsmiling. Victoria had been the most keenly dismayed by Mateo's life choice. More than once she had voiced the phrase, "not living up to his potential." She had clearly seen an Ivy League school as his next step. Pedro looked away, back down the street where Mateo had been just a moment ago.

"Goodbye, my boy," he whispered. Then he added a silent prayer. "May the angels take care of you. And enjoy it all, every bit of it. I'll be with you in spirit."

Mateo made one more stop before he headed down the road to catch the county bus. At the First Congregational Church he went up to the side door, but it was locked. Too bad, a bathroom stop would have been a good idea. The office manager kept later hours, and it was Reverend Prescott's day off. But Mateo was looking for Vic, the organist and a mentor to the boy for many years now. Mateo went around to the front doors of the church, but these too were locked. The only time they were ever locked was when Vic was not there. Vic lived at the church, or close to it. His apartment in town was an address only, a place to shower and keep his extra clothes. The organ and the choir room and the church garden were Vic's habitat. Mateo had spent hours of his youth with this slightly eccentric man who had been a major influence in his life. Mateo wanted to say goodbye. It was unusual for Vic not to be there. Mateo stood, uncertain, for a few minutes. Taking the time to track Vic down at his apartment would mean he might miss his bus.

Mateo moved towards the lane and did not look back. His future lay ahead of him. Instead of leaving home, he felt as if he was going home at last. Like a siren's song the City seemed to call out to him, reaching him even three hours away here in the quiet woods of his home town. By the time he was a quarter-mile past the church, despite the baggage on his shoulders, he broke into a run for the sheer joy of the day.

Vic Dalloway stood hidden in the trees, watching his young friend jog by. He crushed his cigarette under his foot and let the boy go. Life would be less sparkling without Mateo in Pine Junction. Vic felt the emptiness already. But it was the way of the world, the way of youth, and Vic did not have the courage to say this particular goodbye. As Vic bent down to pick up his crumpled cigarette butt, a loud squawk of a blue jay caught him unawares and he jumped, then smiled, and wondered if Mateo had heard the same bird.

7

TELL ME SOMETHING

Olivia

1995 & 1982

"Tell me something I would never guess about you. Something most people wouldn't know."

Brad's gaze was tender. He could not get enough of Olivia's face. Her vulnerability appealed to an unmet need in him. He was in love with her, but more, he had found she was the friend he had always been seeking. Olivia was perfect, from her softly curling hair and emotional eyes, to her gesturing hands, even the colorful dresses she liked to wear. But it was her essential kindness that he honored most.

It was their seventh date. On average they spent six hours per date so he figured they had been together almost forty-two hours. This didn't count the twelve hours he had spent in his capacity as electrician, working on rewiring Olivia's sister's old home in Pine Junction. To his analytical yet romantic mind, those working hours didn't count as relationship, although there would be no dating now, without those hours spent on the ladder running wires through the old lath and plaster walls. Olivia had hovered to make sure he didn't tip off the ladder (a concern he found endearing given his years of experience clambering over and under and on top of old houses all over Western Massachusetts). Olivia and her teenage daughter, Julia, were living with Cecilia at the time, and by his good fortune, it was Olivia who was home the day he parked his truck, hopped up the front steps of the old porch and rang the doorbell, tool kit in hand.

Olivia had the fairest complexion of the three Sanchez daughters. Her sisters, Maria and Cecilia, resembled their father Pedro, with dark eyes and hair. Olivia had her mother's blond looks, from Victoria's German and English heritage, but with a dash of Mexican spice thrown in. Or so this is how the smitten Brad would have described his perfect lady. But no matter the relative merits of her appearance, no one ever disagreed about her warm heart.

Sitting next to him now in the cafe, Olivia relaxed and bloomed in the gentle urgency of this new man, and responded to his question with sincerity.

"Oh my, well, let's see." She wrinkled her nose in thought, and then laughed. "Okay, I bet you would never guess that I won the science fair in fourth grade!"

"No, really? Well, you're very smart. Even then you probably knew you would be a teacher."

"I don't know about that, although it's not surprising with Mother and Papa both being teachers. And I like science, but it was usually my sisters who put themselves out there and entered and won contests. But, that year I had this great project, or so I thought, and I worked very hard on that display board. My parents insisted that I do the whole thing myself, without their help, unlike some others in my class."

"Ah, cheaters, eh?"

"Yes, Tammy Finley and Richard Jameson, my biggest competitors, both had their parents doing research and helping with the art work. I was sure they would win. Their boards looked so much better than mine. So I was absolutely shocked when I was announced the winner. I think I may still have that blue ribbon."

"What was your project?"

"Batteries. I was checking out batteries to see which ones would give the longest lasting power for various purposes."

"So someday you could sit here with an electrician and impress him with your knowledge about energy, is that right?"

As if they had both said something profoundly clever, the two sat there in the unfamiliar cafe, pleased with themselves and oblivious to anyone else. Their location was three townships away from Pine Junction where Olivia was a third grade teacher. It was enough that the whole town of Pine Junction had seen her first marriage dissolve into deception and humiliation several years ago; she did not welcome the prying eyes of her curious neighbors as she launched a new, and perhaps lasting, relationship.

"Okay, your turn. Tell me something that most people don't know about you, Brad."

He thought for a moment. "Well, I never told anyone that I cried when I first learned there was no Santa Claus. Went to my bedroom and cried like a baby."

"Ah, Brad, that's so sweet. My students are half and half, some believing and some not believing but wishing that they still did believe."

Olivia had found that Brad genuinely enjoyed hearing about her third grade students, their personalities and learning styles, her worries and delights with the youngsters in her class. As a contrast, her first husband Kevin had never once in all their courting or marriage inquired about her teaching day or her students. It had taken her fifteen years with Kevin, years of affairs (his), and years of misery (hers), for Olivia to recognize his disinterest in her passion. Once she did though, it was the last straw. If there was anything she took seriously, it was her teaching. Kevin's disregard for her career, combined with his last blatantly indiscreet affair, dealt the final blow to the marriage. At last Olivia Sanchez Howard moved to action and the divorce unfolded. It had not been easy for her gentle soul to undergo.

But now a few healing years later, she was both excited and comfortable to be sitting here with Brad Miller.

"One more, Olivia. One more scene from your life. I want to picture you as a little girl. And then I want to know about your teen years."

Olivia closed her eyes and let herself drift back to her childhood. She thought of the bedroom shared by all three sisters until Maria, the oldest, turned twelve and wanted more privacy, shared simply because the girls liked to be together. She saw herself as a six-year-old. In her memory, she was surrounded by her dolls and stuffed animals.

"I had a whole ritual of saying goodnight to my doll and animal family," she told Brad. "I carefully kissed each one and put them in the doll bed with a blanket up to their chins. Then I read them a story and finally I picked out two or three each night to sleep with me."

She smiled as she recalled holding her favorite doll tightly in her arms and looking down into the painted doll face, with the lashes that closed when the doll was held down horizontal and then popped open when you held her upright. What a thrill it had been to get that doll for Christmas, her first doll not handed down from her older sisters. A baby doll of her own. How she had loved to hold its soft body tightly to her chest.

Sitting close to Brad in the booth, holding hands under the table, her smile suddenly froze, and her body went rigid. Brad felt her hand clutch at his fiercely.

"What's wrong Olivia? Are you okay?" Brad touched her cheek.

Olivia was somewhere else. Brad wondered if she was having a seizure. His younger brother had those kind of seizures where you just sort of disappear into yourself for a few seconds or minutes. So he waited and watched, worried, as Olivia's face went blank.

1982 was the year. Olivia was in the delivery room, head propped on the pillow, weary although the labor had been short and sudden, not long and involved like with Julia, her first-born. In her arms lay her just-born son, Nicholas James. He was still. He would never move, never wave his little arms, or open his tiny mouth in a yawn, or scrunch up his nose, all the little movements Olivia remembered about Julia's first hours. Nicholas was very tiny, perfect, but dead. It was a word Olivia was unable to associate with a baby, her baby, and she had tried to say to Kevin, "our baby," but the words did not come out.

The nurse had placed her son in her arms, after the doctor had brusquely told them that their son was born too early, stillborn, dead. He had the audacity to add, "But you're young, you can have another to give your husband a son."

The veteran nurse glared at the doctor, who soon left. Olivia was unable to fathom what she had just heard. The nurse held her hand and rubbed her arm and cheeks, wisely not saying anything. Kevin just stood there, and then he turned away, looking out the window, never looking at his wife in the bed. When the nurses placed the baby in Olivia's arms so she could hold him, Kevin remained with his back to her.

Olivia held her son and looked at his perfection. She tried to understand how he could look so right on the outside and not be alive, not squirm against her belly as he had for weeks now. She touched his little legs and felt again how they jabbed against her from the inside. Now they were unmoving. She touched his hair. It was dark, perhaps like her own father because both she and Kevin were light-haired. He was her baby, but he was so unlike Julia who had been strong and lusty-voiced from the beginning, moving and reaching at the world from the moment she entered. Nicholas was not alive. She could see that. But she could not grasp this fact. How could he be turning and kicking inside of her so recently, and now so motionless?

Olivia looked up again at her husband. His back was silhouetted against the light of the window. His broad shoulders did not shake. They seemed solid, a barrier opposing her fragility. She started to call his name, to beg him to come and hold her and to be with little Nicholas before they came and took him away, as she knew would happen soon. But Kevin's back stopped her. It was so impenetrable, as it was often in bed at night. In truth, he presented a wall to her, even when he was facing her direction.

Therefore Olivia did not call to him, but she silently willed him with all her might to turn around. "Just turn around, Kevin. Look at me. Look at our baby boy."

Then, Olivia gave up on Kevin and focused instead only on the baby in her arms. She rocked him as if he were alive and needed soothing. Her body shivered and she held the baby tighter, so tight that if he had been alive, he might have been uncomfortable. It was too fierce. The nurse watching the whole tableau from one side of the bed began to be alarmed, gently stroking the grieving mother's arms, trying to help Olivia release the tiny dead baby from her iron grip.

At that moment Victoria walked in the door. She stood for just a second and took in the scene: she looked at the man at the window who barely registered his mother-in-law's presence, and she saw the nurse who, despite her professional calm, looked worried. Finally, Victoria took in the sight of her youngest daughter enveloped in the hospital bed. Olivia's skin had whitened to blend in with the sterile hospital gown and sheets, but in the midst of this paleness, her daughter's eyes blazed out with the only color to be seen, unnaturally wide-eyed, already scarred with fresh grief.

Victoria made herself look at the tiny bundle in Olivia's arms. Her grandson. They had told her the story on the phone, and for the first time in her teaching career, Victoria left work early, not even waiting for her husband to join her.

Without a word, she quickly took the few steps to be beside her daughter and enfolded her in her arms. In her mother's embrace, Olivia began to relax the steel grip she had on the baby, allowing the nurse to breathe a little easier. Victoria helped Olivia hold the preemie infant between them in a more gentle embrace. Olivia had always been the daughter with whom Victoria could feel the most herself, her closest child, and the tragedy of this moment created another connection between the two women going forward. This bond was never articulated in the years to come, but it was well understood by both.

Kevin finally turned around and without making eye contact, he looked at Victoria holding his wife and his dead baby, and then he left the room.

Olivia was shaking now. Even in her mother's arms, she could not stop the violent shuddering of her whole body. Victoria said nothing but kept her arms wrapped tightly around the young woman's shoulders, pressing Olivia's head into her breast. The nurse left the room saying she would be right back with a sedative for Olivia. Victoria silently nodded in agreement, and when she did, the nurse saw Victoria's tears.

For a while after the funeral, everything was fuzzy to Olivia. No one talked much about the little boy lost; perhaps they didn't know how to express their own sadness or meet Olivia's pain. Even young Julia learned to stop asking what happened to her baby brother. Olivia dropped out of her grief counseling sessions, not being able to find how to help herself. In time she went back to work and daily swallowed the permanent lump in her throat.

Emerging from her trance and recalling where she was, Olivia looked at Brad's concerned face. His love enveloped her sadness and soothed the pain. Drying her eyes with a napkin, she noticed Brad was shielding her face from view of the other diners and the curious waitress. His back held off the world. His eyes met Olivia's and she let them hold without retreating. It was a hold that would last because he was not a man to be frightened by tears.

They would talk about everything. Olivia knew she was home, and Brad knew their hours together would become too many to count.

8

THAT FIRST DAY

Rex

2000

After eating his bagel and fruit breakfast at the hotel that morning, Rex found himself so ready to start his new life that he took his coffee along in a travel cup and drove the final two hours to Pine Junction, pulling into the driveway at the old parsonage before 9:30 in the morning. It was a Saturday in the autumn of 2000. The famous New England foliage was beginning its big show, and by the next weekend the roads would be full of sightseers and their cameras.

Rex took the box of items he had not trusted to the movers and walked up to the front door, key in hand. He stood there for a few seconds, admiring the comfortable character of the old home, once the official parsonage of the First Congregational Church, and now his purchased home. Again this morning, he had the same sense of well-being that he had experienced on his first visit to Pine Junction when he had interviewed with the search committee and viewed the exterior of the parsonage, holding hope that he might one day live there. His last house in the suburban community outside Chicago had been functional for his family of four in a way that this house was not, but this old parsonage beckoned Rex to come in and settle. It felt like it might become home. Rex was betting the rest of his career, maybe his whole life, on this hope.

He turned the key and walked in the entry hall way, coat closet on one side, side table topped with an old wooden mirror on the other. Past the entry, the room to the left was the dining room, and the round oak table gave him a place to put down his box. The house was half-full of furniture, and once his own furniture arrived he would need to do some clearing out, but for now Rex did not mind walking into the house in a semi-furnished state. Rex was at a place in his life where history added color to the present. He walked into the kitchen and saw that someone had put a bouquet of garden flowers in a small vase on the table.

"Ah, the church women at work." Rex smiled reflexively. He would later recant that stereotype when he heard that the church organist, Vic Dalloway, had been the giver of the flowers. The kitchen was clean, bare except for the flowers. The window over the sink looked out to the woods, and this pleased Rex.

Three years after he lost Beth to cancer, when he suddenly knew he must move on, his single requirement was to live among trees. Soon after, he had picked up the denominational newspaper, and his eye was drawn to a tiny ad in the bottom corner of the last page. The Pine Junction church was doing a search for a new pastor. He looked it up on a map, and smiled. He wasn't sure if it was God calling or the trees, but Rex quite often saw the divine in nature. Some might have thought him blasphemous, but Rex's spirituality had never been guided by such rigid thinking.

Now almost a year later, he crossed the center hallway, treading on the old carpet and thinking of the hundreds who had walked that hallway: in prayer, in daily tasks, in despair, in sickness, and in hope. Rex knew that he was getting awfully sentimental these days. Without Beth to ground him and his children to keep him busy with in-the-moment life, he had been drifting these last years. He was going through the motions of his life and the motions of his ministry. He knew that. If his suburban congregation had noticed, they were either too polite or too caught up in their own routine ways to comment. Rex knew it was good for them, as well as for him, to leave.

He continued to explore the old house. There was a living room at the front of the house across the central hallway from the dining room. The front window looked out to the street and the side windows framed a fireplace. It was empty of furniture, so his own could fill this room. But it was the next room, separated from the living room by wooden pocket doors, that caught his attention. Rex, an amateur carpenter, admired the warm dark wood and slid the doors open, and then back and forth. Only a little hitch in the slide, and he could fix that easily. The beauty of the wood and the craftsmanship of the doors made Rex feel ridiculously happy.

He walked into the study and smiled at the two full walls of bookshelves on opposite sides of the room. It was really a library. Rex's happiness reached a giddy level. One wall of book shelves was still full of books. The other was empty and recently dusted. Between the two walls was an old-fashioned library table and chair. The windows at the back of the room looked out onto the same woods that he had seen from the kitchen windows, and two comfortable arm chairs sat together where the afternoon sunshine could warm the occupants.

Rex was up close inspecting the book titles when he heard a timid throat clearing and turned around to see a tall, thin woman, older than himself, standing there clasping her hands and looking nervous.

"Hello." Rex offered her his hand. "Rex Randall."

"Oh, hello, Reverend Randall. Welcome to Pine Junction. I'm sorry if I surprised you. I saw the front door was open and thought I would check in to see if you need anything."

Rex smiled in his practiced pastoral manner and prompted her, "And you would be?"

"I'm Mrs. Gregory. Lillian Gregory." She fluttered a bit, and then added, "I was, well, I was sort of a housekeeper to Dr. Prescott when he was here, before we lost him."

At this, her eyes grew far away, and Rex could feel her grief, even though he knew it was four years since Carl Prescott had died during a trustees meeting one evening at the church. The church had gone through several false starts after that, with interim ministers who had not worked out for a variety of reasons. Rex started to dismiss this woman's grief as being overdone, and then stopped himself as he acknowledged that his own grief for Beth, while not playing out in the transparent fashion of this woman, was still ever-present in his heart. In fact, he was no more over losing Beth than Lillian Gregory was over the death of Dr. Prescott. He was just a little more sophisticated about his grief.

"You must miss him very much, Mrs. Gregory. He was with this congregation for many years. One does get to know and love a long-time pastor."

"Oh, yes, Reverend Randall. I will never forget him. Things are not the same without him." She stopped and her thoughts seemed to go back through the years. Then she bit her lip and said, "I cleaned the house here for him and brought him meals because, you know, he was a bachelor like you. I could start coming in several days a week to tidy up here, and I can organize the ladies to bring you meals. Dr. Prescott was especially fond of my chicken mushroom casserole."

Rex, while empathetic, wanted to nip this offer of help in the bud.

"Thank you so much for your offer, and, yes, I'm a widower, Mrs. Gregory, but I'm accustomed to doing my own house-cleaning and cooking too. I find I enjoy cooking very much, especially baking, although I would love to try your chicken casserole sometime if you would be so kind." He smiled a warm smile at the woman and cheerfully motioned his arm to the room of books. "But this is really where I could use your help. Are these Dr. Prescott's books?"

Lillian was distracted from her dismay at a single male pastor who would do his own cooking and housekeeping, and now, reminded of Dr. Prescott's books, she nodded vigorously.

"Oh yes, he loved those books, dear man. He spent every night with his books, and he was so protective, he didn't even let me dust them. So they're probably filthy. I cleaned out some of the shelves and had Tiny get the room ready for you, but I didn't know what to do about these books because they were his favorites, and well, I just couldn't have them tossed, or . . . whatever."

She gazed up at the bookshelves as if the beloved Reverend Dr. Prescott would appear and reach for a dusty book, pipe in hand, and head for his seat by the fireplace, where Lillian would bring him a glass of brandy before she left for the evening. Rex wondered if Dr. Prescott had paid Lillian for her attentive house help, or whether she just offered her services out of devotion and his perceived helplessness as a male. Rex wondered if there had ever been a Mrs. Prescott. He gave Lillian a second look and wondered more about her relationship with Prescott, but as the woman dithered past him to the shelves to take a closer look, he left that thought.

"Mrs. Gregory, perhaps you and someone else from the church who knew Dr. Prescott well can start going through these books carefully and help me decide the best care for them. I love books, too, and there may be many that I would love to read and keep, but some might be best suited for a theological library. We can find them a good home with people who will appreciate Dr. Prescott's important legacy, and others can be dispersed to people like you who were close to him. Would you be willing to help me with that project?"

Lillian Gregory perked up and almost beamed as her hands nervously clasped and unclasped, and she nodded five or six times. Then Rex, with practiced skill, brought the conversation to a close.

"Right now I am going to get myself oriented before my moving van arrives, which will be very soon. I should be ready to meet the office staff and the council at the church tomorrow morning, once I get all my boxes and furniture into the correct rooms here. In a week or so, when I have everything settled, I'll invite the congregation to have an afternoon tea here, and I'll make my favorite lemon cake to share. I do hope you'll bring one of your specialties, too."

As he spoke, Rex ushered Lillian out of the room, down the hallway, and onto the front porch, where Rex commented about the burgeoning color of the maple trees. As she walked through the front gate, Lillian found herself more sure-footed than she had been in a very long time, and her heart seemed to be beating a more normal rhythm. She unclenched her arms, and let her hands hang loosely by her sides and swing with her steps. He seemed unconventional from her experience of ministers, but the Reverend Rex Randall gave her a sense of confidence. She didn't feel quite so responsible, so worried, for the state of affairs at her precious church. After four years of mourning the passing of Dr. Prescott, maybe things would be okay after all in Pine Junction.

Back at the house, Rex carefully locked the front door behind him and went upstairs to check out the bedrooms, three small ones, and single bathroom. It was an old house. He thought of the three bathrooms in his suburban house, and how even with all those bathrooms, sometimes the four of them, his daughter, son, and he and his wife, would be hassled in their morning preparation time. Rex stood in the doorway of the old tiled bathroom and he could hear his kids shouting and giggling with each other, and visualize Beth running in and out of the bathroom, hair brush in hand, half-dressed as she got ready for work. He took an involuntary sharp intake of air. It still hurt.

Yet, here he stood in this lovely old house. He felt only peace as he walked the creaking floors. He was alone now. He did not need all those bathrooms. He didn't need a two-car garage. He only needed a simple kitchen, a comfortable bed, one bathroom, and that classic old library downstairs. A fireplace sounded welcoming for the cold winters ahead. One step at a time, he could live into this new life.

Now he stared out the window of the bedroom, hands resting on the windowsill. From upstairs he could see down the slope to a creek behind the trees that bordered the back of the property. His mind bounced back to Lillian Gregory, his first contact on this his first day in Pine Junction. What was the significance of her presence? Just another older church lady? A caricature? A pathetic old woman?

Rex had been around churches for a long time now. In the beginning, as a long-haired activist, Rex's fiery speaking had matched his auburn red hair. Rex was often in trouble with the religious establishment and civic leaders because of his agitating sermons. He had been arrested, jailed, and still he preached, still he marched, and still he organized. However as enough time passed, he came to be admired even by his detractors, and adored by many as the rising star of prophetic voice and a tireless proponent of social justice and progressive action.

Years on, he further transitioned into serving suburban churches that had fewer budget problems and less street crime to deal with, but demonstrated just as big spiritual needs as he had seen within the less affluent urban churches he once served. In fact, sometimes wealth, which bought security and comfort, made the soulful needs even bigger. What was called for was kinship among different church groups and their communities. He learned, more diplomatically but still strongly, how to bridge the gaps, break down barriers, ignite the flame of service, merge religious faith with political action, and get across the message of justice - to advance the causes he held so fervently. He lost some of his rough edge, but never gave up his push to advance what he believed.

However, after several decades, Rex became fatigued being the relentless prophet crying in the wilderness. Guilt set in. How could he let go of the good causes? What was making him feel like giving up? Finally, one night, with Beth by his side, he collapsed, emotionally at least. After a long night of discussion, he recognized that his message had begun to be driven more and more often by his ego. With shame he saw a degree of arrogance behind his hue and cry, and slowly he began to understand that no matter how faith-based and true he believed his message to be, it had become more about his own outrage and rightness than the needs of the people. He tasted a falsehood in the back of his throat. It was all too much about him, not about his congregants or humanity in general, or about his calling from God, if he really believed in that anymore.

Rex was coming to this humbling revelation about the time Beth became ill; and, for the next two years, she was his centering point while he half-heartedly managed his church work. The congregation was supportive because they loved Beth too; sometimes they had loved her more than Rex. They certainly understood her better. When she passed away, the congregation held each other in their sadness. Neighbors and friends and coworkers of his wife also supported each other. Rex tried to be there for his children, now college students, but felt inadequate. They were as devastated by Beth's death as he was, but somehow they were all separated rather than united by their grief, and Rex felt alone.

He went through the motions at church and meetings. He dutifully kept track of his children at their universities and jobs. But at night he sat in his too-big house, a house that had always been simply functional, and now no longer felt like home. He would wander about and pick up something that had been Beth's and stare at it. Sometimes he would put it down. Sometimes he would hold it all night, even in bed. And occasionally he surprised himself with his anger and would throw the object against the wall.

It did not matter how much theological training he had completed, or how many religious teachings he had absorbed. It did not matter how many words of comfort he had offered to bereaved families, nor how many times he had prayed by the bedside of a man or woman in transition to eternity. It did not seem to mean much now. He could not bear the absence of his Beth. He would break out in sweats as he tried to think about her not being in the world anymore and question what he believed about afterlife, spirit life, the white light of love and eternity. He doubted.

He only wanted his Beth. Beth. He thought of his lovely fleshed-out wife, with her lively mind, cheerful laugh, and warm body with a beating heart and flowing blood, and breath that went in and out of her lungs. He remembered her laughing gently at him across the dining table, as well as groaning in pleasure with first he on top of her and then her on top of him, her breasts such a beautiful sight that even now he could see them and her half closed eyes and radiant face above him. Now, for her to no longer be with him was almost impossible to comprehend; he let his mind grow numb as much as possible because at this point his thoughts disturbed him more than anything had ever frightened him before.

Who were his friends? Where were the connections of fellow pastors? Where was his faith? What should he do? It felt like everything he had formerly been sure about had deserted him all at once. Everything that had fired up his passions, his early ministry and leadership in community work, his lust and love for Beth, the birth of his daughter and then his son, his sense of responsibility for the mission of the church were all stripped away. His belief in his own ability to affect change, his view of his role in the church, the strength of his faith, were - like his children and his wife - all gone.

A few years went by. Rex pounded many nails for Habitat for Humanity. He shared doughnuts and conversation at coffee hour. He chaired meetings of civic groups and preached a sermon each week. He mowed his lawn and took a cooking class. He practically moved into the local library and brought home armloads of books from the bookstores, filling tables and floor space once his own book shelves filled full. He went through a lot of motions. He hoped it would help. And it did a bit. It made a few inches of difference.

And then he knew. He had to leave. He had to change his environment. And hearkening back to his youth in Oregon, he thought of one thing. Trees. I must live among the trees. He walked through his sanctuary one day on a quiet Thursday morning. No one else was there. Rex sat down in a pew in the middle of the church and stared ahead at the stained glass window and the altar. The silence filled him up with a quiet rush. He looked at the pulpit and he thought to himself, "I'm not finished. God is not finished with me. I can start fresh and try to be open to both humility and strength. There is service for me yet. I have more I can do, and I can do it in the life of a church. I want to hear the music. I want to serve and take communion. I want to talk about ideas and faith with people who care enough to show up. I want to dance at weddings and hold babies in baptism. I want to usher children through their lessons, and I want to have rebellious discussions with teenagers that shake up my faith and that of their parents. I want to be with people when they are sick and when they die." Rex stopped and lifted his head up in discovery. "I want to try to learn something that will help me and others understand the mystery of life and death better. Yes, it's time for me to learn from others while I serve them. That's the path for me. I don't have to have the answers. I can't make the answers come. Maybe the answers don't even matter. But I can be open to clarity, and let faith and even hope happen in good time, in God's time, in my time."

As if he had just heard an inspiring sermon, Rex got up from the pew and walked directly to his office. He picked up the denominational newspaper. In the end it was really that simple. He picked up the phone, he filled out his papers, and he waited through the normal process, but he never had a doubt.

And now he stood at the window of his new home. He was on his own, but he didn't feel lonely. He had met a fine panel of congregants at his interview. He knew that Lillian Gregory was but one of many individuals, each one having something to offer. Mrs. Gregory reminded him of so many of the stalwart women of the churches he had served from the inner city to the grassy stretches of upper-middle-class American life. Some out-spoken and confident, others dithering with nervousness, yet with so much to offer. Women who showed up because they cared. And there were others - male and female, young and old - in the congregation here, as in his other churches, who were educated or not, talented or not, kind or crusty, but they all had something to give and something to teach him. Of that he was now very certain.

The sound of a truck braking and parking roused him from his thoughts. He bounded down the stairs to greet his stuff, all the stuff that had accompanied him along his journey and would now mix in with the flotsam and jetsam of Dr. Prescott and long ago ministers here in this house that already felt like a home. He would have little time for musing in the next weeks as he began a new life, but later that winter, on the long snowy evenings, on the nights without church or community meetings, he would sit by his fire holding either his own book or one of Dr. Prescott's, enjoying a glass of brandy or a beer, poured and served with his own hand, not Lillian Gregory's, who would be far too busy as church librarian and archivist of the large Prescott legacy of papers and books, to bother herself with what he ate or drank.

9

A RIDICULOUS NOTION

Derrick

2000

If Pine Junction was located on a train track, Derrick Jackson was born on the wealthy side of the tracks. However, any close observer might have noted that he was born on the wrong side of good fortune. But, sometimes, fortune can change depending upon your luck.

After the long drive up from Florida, Derrick's hands were shaky with more than fatigue as he put his key into the front door of his childhood home. It was a miracle that he had remembered he still had the key tucked away in a tattered cardboard box shoved to the back of his closet. The old box had traveled with him for five years, ever since he fled Pine Junction for good.

Now, key in hand, he was back. Palm Beach to Pine Junction, Florida to Massachusetts. Two opposite universes.

The door opened smoothly. Derrick stood three steps inside the door and looked around. There was no sense of human occupation, which was a relief to him - he had feared the over-powering presence of his father might still be lingering in the house, despite having received official word in writing of his father's death. (Sparsely worded from the attorney: Mr. Jackson found dead in a hotel room in Atlantic City, cause of death suspicious, suicide suspected.) Now Derrick wandered from room to room, and nothing seemed out of place. It was like walking into a hotel suite, absolutely sterile.

Glancing at his watch, he saw that he had one hour until his appointment with the local attorney. A shower or a nap? Afraid that he would over-sleep, he opted for the shower.

Emerging from the bathroom, his father's towel around his waist, Derrick abruptly confronted himself in the full-length mirror on the closet door. Stopped short, he took stock. Blond hair, spiked in all directions by his vigorous toweling, and brown eyes, a "combination which was exotic," Steve had gushed upon first meeting Derrick. Now those eyes were bloodshot. Stubble covered his chin. He was shaving more these days, but yet not being used to this change, he had left his shaving kit in the car. His bare chest sported a layer of sparse fur but it still caught Derrick by surprise, another recent development. His chest and arms were fuller too, muscled, and he reflexively flexed his shoulders and biceps, watching as if it were someone else's body. Derrick had been a late bloomer, and had grown over three inches since high school graduation. What he saw before him, in his father's mirror, was a man. It dawned on him that Steve had wanted the smooth slender eighteen-year-old boy to last forever.

There was something final in this unexpected self-appraisal. And it spelled out for Derrick how crucial this timing was to inherit his father's estate. It was essential.

At precisely three o'clock he was sitting across from Mr. Taylor, his father's attorney. The man's movements were methodical, his voice monotonous. Derrick wondered how old the man was by now. When you are twenty-three, everyone looks older to you. Mr. Taylor explained the situation with Derrick's father's estate, but Derrick's exhausted mind had to ask him to repeat things several times before it sank in that this was not like in the movies where everything that had been the father's was promptly handed over to the son. It seems that there were complications, and whether they were deliberate on Ted Jackson's part - to disinherit his son, or just a matter of procrastinated planning or poor management on the part of the man - was not something the attorney knew or cared to share with Derrick.

In a daze, Derrick left Mr. Taylor without a handshake, and walked out to Pine Junction's Main Street. Seeing a market he crossed the street without looking left or right, something that would have led to his death on the busy Palm Beach streets. He made a few haphazard purchases, coffee, bananas, cheese, bread, candy bars. Checking out, he first dropped and then fumbled repeatedly in his wallet to retrieve some cash. The clerk eyed his shaking hands, as did the man in line behind him. Holding his paper bag close to his chest, Derrick left the store and shuffled slowly back to the house.

A car horn blared and a hand grabbed his arm, keeping Derrick from walking in front of an irritated driver. That was the first Derrick realized that someone was walking beside him down the quiet street. Without saying anything, the man from the store had caught up with Derrick and had been matching him step by slow step. Derrick gave him a furtive glance, the man nodded. No words were exchanged until Derrick turned off in front of his father's house, and placed his hand on the gate latch. Then the man spoke to Derrick's back.

"Having a bad patch of it?"

Caught by surprise, Derrick was horrified to find his eyes filling with tears and his throat too choked to speak. So there was a moment of quiet. Finally, "You could say that."

"I'm not busy. Would you like to join me for some coffee?" The man motioned across the street to the house opposite. Derrick was sure he said no, and he meant to walk into his house or even jump into his car, but somehow he found himself walking across the street with the stranger, still holding his groceries to his chest.

When they got to the front door of the house, the man said simply, "I'm Rex Randall. This is my house."

Derrick's memory woke up. "This is the church house, isn't it?"

"Yes, it was the parsonage for the Congregational Church. I'm the pastor and now it's my home."

He looked at Derrick's alarmed face. "I hope you won't hold that against me."

Derrick did, but somehow when Rex held the door open with an invitation on his face, Derrick walked on in. Rex went to the kitchen and put his own groceries down, then busied himself making some coffee while Derrick stood in the doorway still clutching his paper bag. When Rex finally turned around with two mugs in hand he invited Derrick to sit, and he did. Everything seemed like a dream.

"I don't think this is the best coffee in the world, but I can't seem to get used to this new coffee pot."

Derrick took a sip and without thinking of being tactful, replied, "It's stale and too weak." Then, apologetically. "I'm sorry. I'm so tired I can't remember my manners."

Rex laughed. "I have no pride about my coffee-making, so, thanks for the tip. I'll dump this old stuff and buy some new. I love good coffee but can't seem to get the handle on making it. In fact, I don't think I've had a good cup of coffee at home since my wife passed away." The pastor reflected for a moment before bringing himself back to the kitchen table and his guest.

Derrick knew he should voice some note of sympathy but he didn't have the energy.

Rex looked at the young man and stated, "I'm new here myself, moved here just two weeks ago, so I don't know if I'm talking to a newcomer or a long-time Pine Junction man."

Derrick finally offered, "I'm Derrick, Derrick Jackson. I just arrived here this afternoon. But I grew up here. That's my father's house across the street. Well, it's the house I grew up in, but I haven't been here in years."

"Derrick, good to meet you. I was told by one of my new parishioners that the gentleman who lived there passed away recently. Your father, I suppose. My sympathies to you." Rex didn't mention the scandalous tone with which his parishioner had imparted this information.

Derrick's face clouded further and he felt compelled to confess. "We weren't close. In fact, we hadn't talked in five years. Truthfully, Dad kicked me out five years ago, and we hadn't talked since."

"I see. Yes, that can complicate grief."

That was too much. "I don't give a damn about Dad! The things he shouted at me the last time I saw him are all I can remember. And now he has screwed me again!" Derrick's breath was coming labored now as he vented what he had wanted to shriek so many times in the past but always kept bottled because no one was really interested in his past. So many of the people in his world had pain and rejection in their histories that for the most part they all lived in the present, a flamboyant and delightful present. Not that his acquaintances weren't in their own way caring, but few had the energy to go back and address everyone's past sorrows. So to scream out these childish words in front of this stranger named Rex - Derrick had already forgotten the last name - was therapeutic.

It also brought him to the end of his rope, to his current situation.

"I don't know what to do. I can't go back to Florida. Steve kicked me out for good. And I thought I could sell Dad's house and move somewhere new and start over, but now I don't know what to do, or whether to go on . . . whether to even go on . . . ."

Derrick's voice faded out and his empty eyes stared into the wall behind Rex's shoulder.

Rex nodded. Matter-of-factly he suggested, "I don't have any plans for the rest of the day, I wouldn't mind listening to any part of your story you want to share. Or, if you just want to catch some sleep somewhere other than your father's house, I have a comfortable sofa in the living room. No one will bother you."

Derrick, being too tired to be defensive of his fragile self, found himself directed to the sofa, thrown a blanket, and then left alone. Rex closed the pocket doors in the hallway, and brought his book to the dinner table to read so he could keep an eye on the front door. It was completely quiet for three hours.

When Rex's own hunger came on strong, he quietly moved around the kitchen frying some onions and sausage and eggs. The smell served a purpose and Derrick woke with a start, looking around the unfamiliar room. As he adjusted to his surroundings he heard first one voice and then others, whirling around his mind.

The first was Steve's voice: "You're really annoying me. I've found someone new, someone sweeter. Someone who will do more for me than you ever could. Just pack up and leave."

Then Mr. Taylor's bland tone: "Your father's estate will have to go through probate and that could take a while. The house will probably be yours eventually, but the fact is that Mr. Jackson had considerable gambling debts, and he refinanced the house several times, so there is currently little equity in the house. Even when it becomes yours after probate, you would not gain much out of it if you sold. You can live in it for now but you'll need to pay the mortgage payments and insurance and taxes. You should talk to the bank. As for other property, over the last few years your father sold all his cars, including the Jaguar. They're all gone. The only car he kept was the old Chevy and it was at the mechanic when your father died. Bellweather says it's worthless and he'll sell it for parts to pay some of the money your dad owed him for car repairs, but he'll write off the rest of the debt. Your dad's gun collection he sold last year. Coin collection sold. Stocks, too. You understand there were sizeable gambling debts. Bank accounts are empty. The good news is there are no outstanding debts other than the house payment."

The third voice Derrick heard as he woke up from his nap in Rex's living room was his own, from the phone in the motel halfway between Florida and Massachusetts: "Steve, I'll check out Dad's property and sell the house, then I can come back and pay my own way, maybe take some college courses. I'll drive back in the Jaguar. You'll love it. It's a classic, a real beauty. We'll make it work between you and me."

And lastly, the reply - crude and dismissive: "Derrick, don't call me again. You have nothing to offer me anymore. You're yesterday's plaything. Go fuck yourself."

These voices echoed in Derrick's head as he lay there on the strange sofa, yet somehow he was not as desperate or depleted as he had been before his nap in this calm house. He smelled the onions and realized he had not eaten for what seemed like days, since the tasteless pastry at the motel that morning. So he got up, pushed open the old wooden doors, and found Rex in the kitchen.

Rex set out two plates, then looked at Derrick, who nodded hungrily. In a moment Derrick was shoveling eggs and sausage in his mouth as only a person of his age can do. Rex, who was more than twice Derrick's years, smiled approvingly and ate his own supper more sedately.

With empty plates in front of them, Rex patted his own stomach with satisfaction and then asked, "Derrick, are you a drinking man? I always like a little shot of something after dinner. I have some whisky or brandy to offer."

"I'll drink anything but rum - the stuff gives me bad memories of over-indulgences in my younger years."

Rex hid his smile, and pulled out two glasses and a bottle and motioned to his library. "Pardon all the boxes. As I said, I just moved in two weeks ago and haven't settled everything yet, but I love this room. Has a great atmosphere."

The two men sat in a comfortable silence while sipping the rich drink slowly. When he spoke at last, Derrick's tone was quiet, but his words were full of the bitterness he felt.

"All the people I've ever met connected to church have despised me and told me I'm going to hell. Just to tell you that up front, although I thank you for dinner."

"I appreciate your honesty, Derrick, but I ask you to consider that just as one person is not like every other person, not all churches are alike either. I have no requirement for you to open your soul, now or ever. I just noticed you were hurting and wanted to walk by your side for as long as you needed."

Despite himself, Derrick blurted out, "I hated my dad. My mom left him, us, when I was in 8th grade. She abandoned me to him, saved herself and left me behind, and I had to live alone with that man for four more years before I ran away to Hartford. He yelled me at me every day, never a positive word."

"Do you see your mom?"

Derrick scowled. "No. I was close to her and then she left with another man, and I guess he didn't like kids. Or that's what my dad told me. I got a few cards from her over the years, but never got to see her. Dad was always cursing her and I guess I was caught in the middle between missing my mom and hating her. I was really mixed up. High school was hard, although I had some good teachers. Mr. Sanchez was my favorite. Guess he would be retired by now. You can bet I was hardly popular in high school, being shy and never being able to bring friends home to my dad's house. And . . . I wasn't out yet, but the kids knew I was different."

Rex sighed and wondered how many of his parishioners had known of the pain in the house across the street from the church. He wondered if the senior Jackson had been a member of the church. He would have to check.

"So you went to Hartford, then? To school? To work?"

"I started community college, but right away I met Steve and he told me to leave school and come live with him, and help him." Derrick gave a sharp laugh."Steve was fifteen years older than me, maybe more, he didn't like to talk about his age, and he had a lot of money. I was really impressed, and it was nice to have someone want me, or like me. Of course, you can imagine he didn't want to mentor me in business. He had other uses for me, if I'm going to be really blunt here, Reverend . . . I'm sorry, what's your last name?"

"Randall, Rex Randall."

"Yeah, Reverend Rex Randall, if I'm going to be blunt with you, I was Steve's sex slave. He liked games where he was always the dominant one. I tried to get into it, but sometimes I felt so abused that I would plan to leave him - after all, I had felt shamed in non-sexual ways all my life - but in the morning Steve would be all cozy and would buy me clothes and feed me exotic food, so I would forget about leaving, figured he really did love me and that I could put up with anything. Am I shocking you, Reverend?"

"Do you want to shock me, Derrick?"

Derrick looked abashed. "No. No. I guess I'm being defensive because I expect you'll want to convert me to your religion. Do you have some kind of system to reprogram me?"

"You mean like some sort of box you would enter and I would press buttons and you would emerge whistling at girls or something?" Rex grinned at Derrick, who began to relax. "Derrick, I make no judgment of how you or your friend Steve live, but I'm sure hearing that you feel used. That's what can destroy your spirit. It sounds like you have been wrestling with this feeling for a long time. Did you have a job or other friends?"

"Steve insisted that I not work, so I was home almost all the time. We moved to Florida very soon after we met. Before we left for Palm Beach, I felt bold enough, or stupid enough, to go confront my father with my gayness."

"Is that when he blew up at you?"

"Yes, five years ago. He never contacted me again."

"And did you contact him?"

"After how he talked to me? No! I never wanted to see him again."

"How did you find out about his death?"

"Somehow his attorney tracked me down. That was four weeks ago, but I ignored the letter until Steve got angry with me one day. I had started talking back to him and refusing to always do what he asked. Just subtle-like. But he noticed and that's when he told me had found someone new, younger, more malleable, sexier, I guess."

Derrick grimaced but continued: "I read the lawyer's letter then, and decided that I would come north to check out Dad's house and get my inheritance, and then maybe Steve would respect me. But when I called him from the road, Steve shut me down. For good, it seems."

"Does that make you feel devastated or liberated?"

There was a long pause. "Both, I would say. But also empty. I've been with Steve since I was eighteen-years-old, and I don't know anything else. And now I have no money, only a house that I can't sell, and here I am back in Pine Junction where I swore I would never set foot again. I'm stuck."

"Do you still feel like you don't know whether to go on?"

"No. I guess that sleep helped. But really, Reverend Randall . . . ."

"Please call me Rex. . . ."

"Rex, I don't know what to do next."

"An exciting time."

"What are you talking about?"

"I'm not mocking you, Derrick. When you hit rock bottom it can be an exhilarating climb upward. The future has so many possibilities."

Derrick glared at Rex.

"Okay, before you slug me, let's find out something. When you were with Steve, how did you spend your time, outside the bedroom? Did you just lie around the pool all day or did you have things to do?"

Derrick reluctantly examined his recent past life.

"I cooked for us, and for parties. Steve threw lots of parties, business and social. The first thing I learned to make was coffee - Steve was very particular about that. The rest I taught myself by watching the caterers until I was as good as they were. That's when Steve quit hiring caterers because I could do a better job. We had a huge kitchen with all the toys and tools. Once or twice a week, I would go to the public market and buy wonderful stuff to cook with. I got to know all the vendors and they would save their best fruits and vegetables for me, and seafood, too."

"Impressive."

"And, I organized all his parties, too; some were huge, on the phone for hours, double-checking, doing set-up, trouble-shooting. Yeah, I did like that. Liked the people and hanging around and joking with them. Felt good when everything went well."

"I'm sure Steve appreciated that."

"He never told me so, but he always had me do the next party, and the next."

Derrick continued, "I did his books, too, although I suspect he kept two sets of books - one legal, which I did, and one a little shady which he paid people to take care of for him." He thought a moment. "And I could make drinks. Everyone loved my cocktails. I didn't drink much myself so I could stay behind the bar all night serving others."

By this point Rex was grinning at Derrick, but didn't say anymore.

A smile slowly spread across Derrick's face, the first Rex had seen; a very handsome young man he was, too. "Well, I suppose I do have some skills and experience, but I could hardly ask for a letter of recommendation from Steve."

"True, true, but at least you have the confidence to put yourself forward. So, let's see what else do you have going for you today? You have a roof over your head for the immediate time anyway, right? Even if it is in Pine Junction and not Miami. And do you have enough money for some food to eat? You do have quite an appetite. And you seem to have a car. Is it yours?"

"It was given to me, but it's not in my name, so Steve may come and repossess it."

"Not with violence, I hope?"

"Hope not, either."

"Well, at least you'll have it for awhile, but there's bus service if you need it. Not too many jobs in Pine Junction, however Amherst is close by, just a thirty-minute drive as you know better than I do, I'm sure. You lived here for your first seventeen, eighteen years?"

"Yeah, I do remember. But. . . " Derrick paused.

"But what?"

". . . it's been a long time, well, in fact, never, since I applied for a job, so I'm not even sure how to go about it."

"You're borrowing trouble for the moment, worrying about that, Derrick. You must be worn out. You've had a long day." Rex picked up his remote control and held up a DVD jacket for Derrick to see. "Have you seen this Ken Burns documentary on baseball, Derrick? I like baseball and have been waiting for a good night to watch this. I'd love some company if you are interested, and after that, I need to call it a night."

Before Derrick could respond, the phone rang. Rex picked up the phone by his chair and listened for awhile.

"June, I'm really sorry to hear this news. Can I do anything for you now? No, okay, glad your kids are there with you." He listened some more. "I appreciate your worry about your work, but right now you need to just worry about recovering. No, no, your job is my responsibility and the council. How long did the doctor say you should stay off work? Six months. Yes, I know that seems very long to you, but remember the old truth - you have to take care of yourself or you're no good to anyone else. Okay, June, no, no, please don't think you let me down, accidents happen to all of us. Take care of yourself, and goodnight to you, too."

Rex put down the phone and thought for a long moment. Then he looked straight at Derrick.

"Derrick, do you think you could handle little old church ladies and gentlemen who might look meek and nervous or sound bossy and opinionated, but are in fact wonderful and fantastic tigers in their spirits?"

"What are you talking about?"

"And, do you think you could help organize my church office? June is a sweetheart but at my first look, the files are kept under a system that frankly baffles my mind. Plus, she is very uncomfortable around a computer and I can already see she is avoiding it like the plague. It's 2000 and we have to get up and going on computers."

"Who's June?" Derrick looked bewildered.

"June O'Keefe, our church secretary, rather, office manager. Been there forever and is a jewel of a woman, but getting a little shaky behind the desk and now she just let me know that she slipped and fell in her kitchen and has broken several bones. She's been advised by her doctor to take a long home rest, up to six months. She's absolutely loyal to the church and feels like she is abandoning me just as I arrive in town."

Derrick looked at Rex and snorted. "Are you suggesting that I step into this June's shoes and work in a church office? Me? Me and my gayness in a church office answering the phone and doing whatever else . . ." His face was incredulous.

"That's exactly what I'm suggesting, Derrick. When something so coincidental happens like this - meeting you today and hearing your story, and my office manager calling to tell me she's going to be out for six months - well, I take it as a higher power at work. You can call it whatever you like to call it. And, of course, you can laugh me off as a fool and go home. I'm confident you'll figure something out soon. But, hey, if you make good coffee and organize the church files and welcome folks to our church office with some degree of grace and efficiency, I can give you a good reference for your resume, and in six months your probate may be settled, and then you can do what you will with the house and go off to a new job and a new future." Rex added, "And church attendance is optional."

Derrick sat in a stupefied silence. And then he made one more effort to repudiate this ridiculous notion.

"Rex, I just admitted to you that I have basically been a kept man, a sex slave, and, worse yet in most Christians' eyes, a homosexual sex slave, and just because I'm leaving Steve behind, my sexuality does not change."

"Of course not, Derrick, now you're being ridiculous. Who would think that? I'll have to chat with the church council and they may have someone else in mind, but you're a local man and it's a chance for the congregation to prove that they are as open as they claim to be. Since you'd be a substitute and you'll be on your way in six months to take on the world, start that restaurant, build up a business or whatever strikes you, I don't have much doubt that if you want to make a go of this church job, it could be yours. It doesn't pay much so think of it as a building block for your resume, an internship of sorts. I'll certainly push for it, as long as you could give me a sign of commitment for just six months."

Six months later, June the Secretary retired to her daughter's in Virginia, forty years of service well-honored by the congregation. Derrick was begged by the church council and parishioners to stay on "just a little longer." Probate remained unresolved for Derrick to inherit his father's home, a house with no equity but one that had already lost its cold and haunted atmosphere. Between the small income from the church and weekend employment with a catering firm in Amherst, Derrick managed to pay his mortgage and bills. The church folks kept him well-fed. Derrick began to work on some personal resolution regarding his father's anger and addictions. He also made an initial contact with his mother in Texas. Steve sent Derrick the pink slip to his car as a gesture of guilt, or perhaps some humanity.

Derrick also began a friendship with James Chui, the youngest son of the local Chinese restaurant owners, and the two shared James's excitement for future remodeling of the old cafe to something new for Pine Junction, whenever James finished his business degree and his parents finally stepped away from their grill and wok. It is a possibility that James and Derrick were beginning more than a friendship, but they both agreed to take it very slowly and tenderly.

And Rex began enjoying good coffee as he settled into his new life in Pine Junction.

By 2007, six years later, Derrick finally went from full-time to part-time at First Congregational Church so he could partner with James on their long-anticipated dream of creating a destination restaurant in Pine Junction. The elder Chius were nervous about these changes, but James and his sisters encouraged them to take the first vacation of their lives out to Seattle for an extended visit with James's oldest brother Martin. There the senior Chius began to relish their role as grandparents to Martin's two children. The old house across from the parsonage, now in Derricks' ownership, had shed its sterile look and all guests remarked on its distinctive charm. There was some equity built up in the mortgage by now, but Derrick had no plans to sell. Pine Junction was home.

10

QUEST

Javier

2004

During his summer break from the University in 2004, Professor Javier Jimenez spent some time in his home town. Phoenix in summer can be relentlessly hot, but the heat of Phoenix this particular week seemed doubly oppressive, especially as each day passed and he wandered in fruitless pursuit of his father. Unlike his usual precise self, he started out each morning with no clear agenda, driving aimlessly into his old neighborhood that once was its own small town, but now had become encircled by the out-of-control growth of the sprawling city.

On the third day, Javier entered the Cold Spot bar on Mesa Road. It was not the type of establishment the mathematician normally patronized, but he remembered it from his childhood and had often wondered what went on behind the weathered swinging door. Enticed by the name on this hot day, he walked in, blinked as his eyes adjusted, and made his way to the bar where he ordered a Dr. Pepper first, then changed his mind and asked for a very cold beer. The good Mexican beer on tap had been one of his mother's favorites.

Javier sat for some time looking down at the beer that had been delivered without comment by the bartender. Mexican music played in the background, Mexican Muzak, thought Javier. Across the bar, the bartender sized him up curiously out of the corner of his squinted eyes. Javier did not match the style of the Cold Spot's usual customer.

The cold beer tasted good, and Javier ordered another. While the bartender filled his glass from the barrel, a man sidled onto the tall stool next to Javier with a great deal of commotion, grunts and sighs, finally settling onto the ripped plastic cushion with a loud fart to emphasize his arrival. The impeccable Dr. Jimenez glanced quickly at his neighbor and then averted his eyes, moving ever so slightly in the opposite direction from the intruder. The long bar was empty of customers, most of the afternoon drinkers being engaged around the pool table across the room. Javier would have expected the man to pick a stool providing a larger buffer zone between two drinkers.

The man was older, probably in his seventies or eighties, but it was hard to tell, given the toll alcohol and too much sun had taken on his weathered skin. He called out his drink order and then turned and looked directly at Javier, who was staring straight ahead.

"Name's Robert. Roberto Garcia." He stuck his hand practically into Javier's face, and Javier had no choice but to turn his body so he could meet the handshake, which was weak and sloppy.

"Javier Jimenez." The reply was curt, and a more socially aware man would have read it as a clear lack of invitation to conversation, but not Roberto Garcia.

By this time, the bartender had returned with the beers and set them down in front of the two. He moved away, but not too far, detached but listening.

"Jimenez. Jimenez? Hm. Not too many Jimenez around this neighborhood these days. Only one I remember, but she bit the dust a few years ago, that slut Celina Jimenez.

Ha! Remember her, Joey?" He turned to the bartender with a sloppy grin and made a sexual motion with his hands.

If Javier had not been in such a tired trance, he most likely would have struck the man for this insult to his mother, punched first and thought about it later. But he was in slow motion this afternoon and just stared at the man. This pause gave him the opportunity to contemplate whether this repulsive old man might in fact know something about his mother in her younger days.

But before he could offer to buy the man another beer to see if he could wheedle some information out of the alcohol-soaked memory, the bartender ordered Roberto to move down the bar and watch his language.

With a shrug Roberto slid off his stool with less fanfare than he had taken to mount it, and lurched off to the pool table to lean in too close to the young woman playing there. She must have known him because she pushed him off nonchalantly and kept on with her game.

The bartender came back to Javier and apologized for the other man's offensive talk.

"Thanks. I should have punched him but he is not worth the effort, an old drunk like him. That was my mother he was insulting. Do you suppose he knew her?"

Javier stretched out his hand to meet the hand of the bartender - Jose was his name. He took a breath and then decided to go on.

"My name is Javier Jimenez. I am here in Phoenix looking for some information about my mother, and, well, other bits of ancient history . . . . " Javier fumbled a bit with how much to share with the bartender.

Jose went back to polishing a glass with a thread-bare white cloth, unsure whether to speak in English or Spanish with this refined-looking Mexican-American man. English, he decided.

"Hard to say with Roberto. He's been around a long time but his memory is spotty and his intelligence wasn't too good to begin with." Jose laughed at his own joke, and looked at Javier with unmasked interest. "Whatcha want to know?"

Javier took a long drink of his beer to stall as Jose wiped the bar thoughtfully, all the while keeping tabs on the whole room with a practiced eye. It was a shabby bar in a poor part of town, but Jose hadn't stayed in business for all these years without some skill at the fine art of hosting, and knowing when to call someone's night.

Javier was trying to figure out how to share the subject of his search when Jose turned back to Javier and mentioned a possibility. "Ya know, there is someone a little more reliable who might be able to help you. He's as old as the desert, but he doesn't drink too much and lived in this neighborhood before I was born. Maybe he could help you. He's a smart man."

Javier perked up and encouraged the bartender to continue.

"Tomàs Garcia is his name. No relationship to that shit-face, Roberto, fortunately. Tomàs comes in every day about 5:00 for dinner."

Javier looked around the place. He hadn't seen any sign that this bar was, in fact, also a restaurant.

"Nah, only for Tomàs. My wife makes him a special meal every day because he is her tio, an honored uncle in her family. So he comes in and sits at that table over there, by the corner. He eats and has one beer, and he comes to tell me to thank Juanita and then he puts on his hat and leaves. Every day. Well, most days anyway. Some days he goes to the track and bets on the horses. You never know." Jose laughed. "Says if he strikes it rich, he'll reward Juanita for all the good meals and tells me then I can sell this joint and go live in Vegas!"

"That would be nice," Javier replied politely.

"Yeah, sure. I guess. I mean it would be different, but I've kind of gotten used to this life here. What would all these people do to get out of the hot sun and have some fun if I closed my doors? So, probably just as well Tomàs doesn't win at the races."

Javier brought him back to the purpose of meeting with Tomàs. "I'll come tomorrow to talk with him, with Tomàs then. Five o'clock?"

"Yeah, sure. He might know something for you."

Jose moved down the bar to serve a new customer and left Javier to ponder if this was another pointless dead-end or something that would pay off. He had only a few more days before he needed to get back to New Mexico. He shouldn't have to worry about his youngest son Armando being home alone at his age, but he never quite trusted that things would go smoothly with the young man.

The next day, Javier slept in after a night of tossing and turning to the sound of the air conditioner churning out a questionable coolness into the inexpensive motel room. His own frugality, born of a childhood of poverty, would not allow Javier to pay for a more deluxe hotel. The drunk's words about his mother hurt more the longer he thought about them. Consider the source, he kept saying to himself, but, nonetheless, it was his mother the crude voice had vilified, and his mother was several years gone now. She had been a good soul at heart, Javier knew that.

After a day spent doing pretty much nothing and feeling quite lethargic in the 110 degree heat, Javier made his way to the old Cold Spot Bar at 5:00. By 5:30, Tomàs had not arrived. Jose shrugged his shoulders and said, "He must be at the tracks. We never know."

Javier wondered what Jose's wife did with the dinner she prepared for the old man and then wondered if the bartender had made up the whole story. Yet, despite his misgivings, Javier spent another idle day and showed up the following day at 5:00 again. Again, no Tomàs. Again, a shrug from Joey.

"I really should go home," Javier said to himself. So why didn't he? The following day he arrived for the third time at the bar right at 5:00. This time he was greeted by Juanita with two plates of steaming food in her hands. She was as outgoing as Jose was reserved, and greeted Javier like a long lost brother, despite having never seen him in her life. She motioned with her head, and a friendly smile, for him to follow her to the corner table where an elderly man sat quietly.

"Here he is, Tomàs, Javier."

Javier wasn't sure if she was introducing him to the old gentleman, or whether it was the other way around. He reached out to shake the old man's hand, and slowly the wrinkled hand moved up to meet his. The old man's eyes revealed little, but while there was nothing said, no gratuitous welcome, somehow Javier did not feel rebuffed so he sat down across the table, and Juanita put a plate in front of him as well as in front of Tomàs. When Javier questioned her, she just shushed him and told him to eat.

"You look like you haven't had a good home-cooked meal in many years," she scolded him, and while this should have elicited a sharp stab of grief for his dead wife's good cooking, somehow it didn't. Javier smiled at her and picked up his fork.

For some time, the old man and Javier ate in companionable silence. When his plate was empty, Tomàs stopped, took a long drink of beer, wiped his face with his napkin and sat contented a while longer. Javier felt peaceful, full of good food, and didn't rush his questions. Some of the old man's serenity had oozed across the table and into Javier.

"You are Celina's son." Finally the old man spoke. Not a question, but a statement.

"Yes." A pause."Did you know my mother?"

"Oh yes. We grew up together. Do you know Spanish? May I speak in Spanish?" Javier nodded.

"Celina and I were neighbors as children before I moved away. We were friends once. Just friends, no more, but that was fine. I left Phoenix for twenty years, and that must have been soon after you were born. Your mama was a good woman, just a girl really, with a good heart. Too trusting a heart, in fact, and it did not enhance her life as it should have. For pure goodness, she should have been rewarded with more than abuse, poverty, a sleazy reputation, and too many children. I'm sorry, but it's true."

Javier nodded, not offended, and Tomàs continued.

"Yes, in a different sort of world, she would have been rewarded with kindness and softness and an easier life. But, as you know, that's not the kind of world we live in. What she had in sweetness, she did not have in good judgment. Such a shame. And then there was the horrible business of the killing. I was gone, but heard word of what happened. What a shame, what a horror for all of you, but she was protecting you all when she stabbed that predator, which I suppose you understood even then. So out of character for Celina to be violent, or to even be brave. But she loved her children more than she feared retribution, at least that time she did."

The old man stopped and contemplated his memories, while Javier considered what this man had said and savored the compassion in Tomàs Garcia's representation of his mother. It gave some atonement or relief to the mixed feelings Javier had long carried about his mother.

"Oh, yes, dear Celina, she let man after man come into her heart and into her bed because she responded to their desires and needs, but she was not strong with them, and so they abused her and threw her away, always leaving their seed with her. How many children did she have, Javier?"

"There were eight of us. I was the oldest."

"Yes, I knew you were the oldest. I remember your birth. I saw you as a baby before I moved to California."

Javier almost stopped breathing at this point. He did not rush the narrative, but he knew it was a pivotal moment.

"Señor Garcia. I have never known who my father was." He stopped trying to know how to ask the question he most wanted answered.

"She never told you?" Tomàs seemed surprised, the most emotion he had shown on his lined face.

"No. She told me that he had died in action, as a hero. But when I got older I realized that given my birth date, that could not be true. I was conceived after the war was over. As a teenager, I confronted Mama on that, but she would not say more. I believe that on her death bed she wanted to tell me, but she slipped away before she could."

Javier looked into the eyes of the man across from him at the small corner table in this run-down bar. "Señor Garcia. Do you know who my father is? Was?"

"Oh yes, Javier. He was a man who had survived much and yet had big dreams. His name was Sanchez, Pedro Sanchez. He was a local young man, raised here by parents who abused him. Terrible life for a child. Sometime after the war his family all left and went back to Mexico, or maybe it was Los Angeles. I don't know. No one really wanted to know, a worthless family. But Pedro was different. And he was in the war, Javier. I don't know if he was a hero, but I do know he didn't die in the war because he came here and met Celina. Well, I don't think he knew her but just the one night, if you know what I mean. Next day he left. What he knew about that night, about Celina, about you, I don't know. Where he went, I don't know. I have no idea. I have no idea how you would find out. It's a big world."

Javier felt like a tornado was going through him. Was this all true, this meeting, this man, this story? Did he really have a father who had a name, a background, a story of his own?

"Pedro Sanchez. Yes, pretty common name." The old man spoke the words Javier was thinking.

Javier looked at Tomàs and, like an angry teenager, burst out, "This is true? You are telling me the truth? You have not invented this story, have you? I need to know that this is the truth, and not a joke. Do not tell me a story, an untruth."

Even in his anger, Javier's words were precisely uttered, and were absorbed without a flinch by the older man. Javier's face reflected the shock of the news and the pain of the years of loss, and this is what Tomàs Garcia could see. This elegant middle-aged man was still a fatherless child.

"Yes, my son. It's the truth that I know. You see, I was at the house that night when Pedro came over. Some of my friends had been school friends of his, so he had stopped by. That's where I met him, first and last time. He seemed to be at loose ends, restless, depressed. Understandable. He had returned from the war, lost a good friend, didn't want to spend time with his own family, and so he came over to drink with us. But he was not able to relax. I remember his name because after he left to go walking with Celina that night, his friends told me who he was and some things about him, the war and a tragedy in his family too, but I don't remember any details. Why do I even remember his name after all these years? I don't know. I have forgotten many things, and yet I remember the name of a stranger all these years later. Perhaps I remember it because it was important that I be here today to tell you this information."

Javier wanted so much to believe that he had discovered the name he had searched for. But he needed to push a little more to make sure he wasn't disappointed.

"So, you say this man went home with my mother, with Celina. How do you know that, well, that I was the outcome of that night? It was just one night, you know, and I know my mother's reputation with men. There could have been someone else maybe, right before or afterwards."

"Good point, Javier. I suppose that a man always wonders about these things. One of the few advantages a woman has over a man in this world, eh?" A very small smile creased his face.

"But Javier, Celina confessed to me afterwards that she had told Pedro that she was eighteen so he would sleep with her, when in fact she was just sixteen and had not slept with a man before, other than a grandfather who had molested her when she was a child. But he had died. Her parents were gone and Pedro stayed the night. It all began for her with that night. She told me that she was pregnant, she said she knew within two weeks because she began to be sick to her stomach and feel different. It was not easy for her because she was all by herself. Her parents tried to help at first, but then her mother died, and her father disappeared. Oh yes, one sadness on top of the last. One time I suggested that she find the man who had got her pregnant and make him take care of her and the baby, but she said no. She said that he had plans to do many great things and that she did not want to make him take care of her and the baby. She said she had deceived him with her age, and she would not tell me anymore or do anything to get help from him. She had a sense of honor, your mother, but I'm not sure her pride resulted in the best decision."

Javier listened with pain.

"I moved away for a long time right after you were born, Javier. My uncle needed me to come to California to work in his nursery, so I left and only returned a few years ago. So, I never saw you grow up nor did I see all the hardships I heard your poor mother endured, granted, many of which she set herself up for by her open-heartedness and lack of judgment. I'm sorry, perhaps I speak too critically about your mother, God rest her soul."

"No, no, Señor Garcia. I think you understood her very well indeed. She was not strong or smart, but she was honorable in her own way, and compassionate." Javier smiled a sad smile. "I wish you had been around when I was grow-ing up, Señor Garcia."

"I'm sorry I have nothing more to tell you about this man who I'm quite positive is your father, Javier. But I hope it's at least a name for you to pursue."

"It is more than I have ever had in my entire life. I am grateful."

"Have you thought about what you will do with this information? And, if you ever locate this Pedro Sanchez, have you thought about the effect on his life when you drop this news on him?"

Javier stared at the old man. He didn't say anything because he had never given a thought about anything but his own need to know. Stubbornly he shook his head.

"I will worry about that when the time comes. If the time comes. No, when the time comes that I locate him."

"Javier, I hope you do give it some thought. This is a big thing, you know. I'll regret ever sharing what little I know with you if there's not a good outcome." Tomàs looked less like a sage for a moment, and more like a worried man. But he continued, more to himself. "But, in a situation like this, I have no choice but to share my little piece of infor-mation that might help you on your quest." Then he added directly to Javier, "Just be kind and be careful, please."

Tomàs slowly pushed himself away from the table and rose to his feet, grabbing his cane off the back of his chair. He turned deliberately towards Javier. When he had been talking he had seemed ageless. Now, as he moved, he be-came again an old man, limited by his aging body. Javier

stood up with him, as good manners demanded. The old-
er man put out his hand and met Javier's own. Tomàs held
Javier's grasp in his own for a time and looked long into
Javier's eyes.

But he spoke no more words, just released Javier's
hand and turned to make his slow way to the bar, where
he spoke to Jose to give his thanks to Juanita for the fine
meal. He placed his hat down on his head, and he made
his way out of the bar into the evening light, needing to
stop to adjust to the brightness before he moved off slowly
down Mesa Street.

Looking after him, Javier stood where he was by the
table until Jose came over to pick up the empty plates and
glasses.

"Find out what you were looking for? Old Tomàs able
to be of any help to you?"

"Yes," Javier managed to say.

"Looked like you were having a pretty serious
discussion."

If Jose was fishing for more information, he was subtle
and Javier missed it. Juanita would want to know more,
Jose knew she would grill him, but it didn't look like he
was going to get an explanation.

Javier seemed to wake up from a daze at this point.
He clapped Jose on the back, almost dislodging the plates
from the bartender's hands.

"Yes, Señor Garcia was a big help. Thank Juanita for
the excellent food - as good as my wife used to make."
Javier started for the door, and then turned back to the

bartender. "And, say, while you are at it, buy that old drunk, the other Garcia, a beer on me next time he wanders in. He may have started a chain reaction of good fortune. But tell him if he ever, ever, slanders the memory of Celina Jimenez again, I will come back with my three sons and put his lights out!"

Javier handed Jose a twenty dollar bill, waved to him and walked out of the bar, turning his father's name over and over in his mind like a perfect pebble.

11

ANGEL IN THE NIGHT

Catherine

2005

The girl was ten years old and the horse underneath her was a veteran mare who knew a novice when she felt one perched on her back. With no malice, but more boredom, the horse took the child for a miserable ride. The jolts from their unsynchronized movement jarred the girl from her butt up through her back and her arms, and on down each finger which gripped the saddle horn in a death grasp. On and on, she was jolted up and down. Then suddenly, the girl was overcome by the sound of an air horn, loud and unrelenting, like a ship's blast to clear the waves in front of its prow.

It was that insistent noise that caused her eyes to open, only to hear what accompanied the jolting - the horrifying shriek of metal meeting concrete at 70 miles per hour. All this drowned out the lovely Dvorak string trio, the very music which had contributed to Catherine's sleep.

As the horn continued to blare, Catherine's eyes popped opened to see her death in front of her against a massive concrete wall. She retained no memory, then or later, of how she moved the steering wheel so quickly to straighten out the trajectory of her father's car, and therefore cruised by her death with centimeters to spare. The right rear view mirror ripped off and went sailing off into the night-time freeway. Seriously damaged from where she had driven over concrete abutments along the side of the freeway, the car at last came to a stop a good hundred yards beyond the overpass.

Clutching the steering wheel, unable to let go, her heart pounded with adrenalin, and she sat there staring straight ahead. Although it was 2:00 in the morning, the freeway approaching New York City held a steady stream of cars and trucks zooming by, their red tail lights forming a blur of receding crimson. Catherine's eyes blinked once and then opened again. Not all the lights were disappearing into the distance. Now red lights were coming backwards, growing larger and brighter right in front of her. Was she coming or going? Where was she? She must be unconscious, she thought. Like Mateo. Mateo, her boyfriend lying in a coma in the hospital back in Western Massachusetts. Like Mateo, Catherine had apparently lost touch with reality.

The Dvorak played on, and Catherine sat stock still. In this rigid state, she nonetheless noted the sound of one, two, three, and then four car doors slamming and what seemed like a crowd of figures approaching and surrounding her car. Voices. But she could not move. Louder voices. Finally a knock on her window. Her eyes could not move from her forward-locked vision, nor could her hands unclench from the wheel. The door beside her opened and when it did, the car light like a merciless spotlight illuminated a face that pushed its way beside her. She turned slowly as if it were a complicated process and saw huge brown eyes, glistening soft and moist in the overhead light. Now, her attention was transfixed by those eyes, under the eyelids, heavy with lashes, closed halfway, still holding her in view. She became aware of rough voices outside the car. But the eyes and their owner overshadowed the voices. The man grinned at her, and she took in the sight of his teeth flashing white like ivory. Her eyes dared to look further, an inch at a time. Splendid dreadlocks surrounded his face and disappeared down his shoulders and back. Everything about this man was large, and, at that moment, beautiful.

"Hey, white girl, you sure almost bought it! Thought we were going to see some kind of fucking big smash for sure. Tried to warn you, but how you drove around that wall I don't know! Thought we'd come back and check it out."

Catherine just looked at him, still unable to move or speak, and he added, "Terrance is my name. You're one frozen chick. Hey, you need a drink."

With that he held out a brown bag from which he first took a drink himself. Catherine looked at her hands, still clinging to the steering wheel. Her eyes willed that grip to loosen and let go. It took an effort but at least she moved her hand to receive the bottle. In an incongruent act of gallantry, the man pulled the bottle back and with long fingers wiped the mouth off with his sweatshirt, before putting it in Catherine's shaking fingers. She lifted it to her lips and with an uncoordinated gulp swallowed deeply, only to gasp and choke with the strength of the brew.

Terrance laughed a deep melodious sound. "That'll put some color back into your face, white girl." He motioned to the CD player. "What the hell kind of music is that?"

At the word music, something clicked in Catherine's brain. "My cello!" She choked out, taking off her seat belt and jumping out of the car in one surprisingly strong movement. Pushing past Terrance and the other men, she pulled open the back car door and falling to her knees pulled her cello off the floor where it had fallen in the near collision. She opened the case and those fingers which had a moment before been like claws, became the sensitive hands of a doctor, examining her precious instrument with expert touch. The men, in various stages of high from a night of socializing, watched, temporarily distracted by the strange behavior they were observing.

Giving a huge sigh, Catherine closed the case on her cello and put it back up on the seat. She turned around and saw five men looking at her, including the tall man with the soft eyes. She was too dazed to feel frightened.

She looked at her car and then looked back down the freeway to the overpass she had just missed. It came back to her. She tried to walk back to the driver's seat, thinking she had to drive on, but stumbled against the open door, shivering as if it were not a humid summer night. Now heaving and shaking, she was in a time-and-space-warp.

Then Catherine was enveloped in warmth, and it smelled like everything at once, and yet nothing specific she had ever smelled before. The aroma was Terrance. She did not immediately know why she was now warm, but without recognizing what she was doing, she pulled the big sweatshirt he had draped on her shoulders more closely around her body. Catherine was not a small woman, but she was dwarfed in the shirt.

"Your car's not going to drive nowhere. Where d'ya live? We'll take you home."

Catherine found she could not speak, so Terrance called off possible towns and neighborhoods until she finally was able to nod affirmatively to the neighborhood where her parents lived, where they were at this hour turning over on their beds and wondering when she would return.

When the men heard where she lived and that Terrance planned to take her home, mutterings spread among them, which, had Catherine been of her normal mind, would have worried her. But she was numb and beyond being wise or foolish, unable to do anything else but nod once again, still speechless.

Terrance pointed her to his car, and Catherine took one step before turning around and opening the back door of her father's car and pulling out her cello, and, as an afterthought, her backpack. Terrance reached in and turned off the engine which was still running, silencing the music. In the silence that followed, he handed Catherine the keys. The freeway roar became the dominant sound along with the muffled conversation of the men she was now following. Later she remembered only pieces of this time.

Enveloped in the huge hooded sweatshirt, she walked forward and saw the car doors of the old Lincoln Continental open in kamikaze style, and soon she was sitting in the middle of the front seat beside Terrance, her cello being held in front of the man sitting next to her by the passenger door. She clutched her backpack on her lap, her arms wrapped tightly around it.

Terrance handed her his brown-bagged bottle, but this time she shook her head, so, he stuck it between his legs at his crotch, and slowly eased the big cruiser onto the freeway. As he was doing so, he saw the name tag on her backpack with her Brooklyn address.

"Hey, you live in Brooklyn?"

"No. My parent's house. Their car. I borrowed it. Have to tell them." She spoke barely above a whisper. The man to her right started swearing to Terrance. "You want to take this bitch to her Daddy's house and have him come out with a shotgun? You're crazy, man. Let's drop her off here on the road or take her with us . . . !"

A chorus of agreement rang out from the back seat where three men had crammed in together.

Terrance pulled off the road.

Catherine looked at him fearfully, now realizing her situation.

"Go ahead and get out, motherfuckers. I'm taking her home."

When no one opened a door or said anything, Terrance started the car up again and for the next hour Catherine sat still, spell-bound, listening to decidedly un-Dvorak music on the car's system, and it occurred to her that Mateo would have appreciated this band. All the while she was wondering whether she was still dreaming. With her mind not working, her senses were working overtime and when she inhaled this man next to her, she decided it was real: a deep sweaty, alcohol and marijuana-infused smell that was not at all distasteful.

Her parent's neighborhood was sedate at 3:30 in the morning when the big silver Lincoln pulled up, the loud music being the only sound to be heard. The men in the back seat shifted uneasily, their eyes looking through the open car windows into the darkness with a mix of hostility and fear. Only Terrance seemed unaffected by being a black man in what he assumed was a white neighborhood. He got out of the car and helped Catherine slide out past the steering wheel. He reached in for her cello and handed it to her. Her well-practiced reflexes balanced both her backpack and her cello gracefully, and she looked at her childhood home like it was an oddly foreign sight. Before she walked away, she turned and looked at the shining eyes of the man. He looked at her, looked up and down the street, then back at Catherine.

"Thank you." She managed to say. And added, "Terrance." And then, "That was you honking at me, right?"

"For a long time, yeah. Damn, you were drifting on and off the road like a mad dog, your car bouncing, thought it might come apart. Thought you were a goner when you headed for that wall. It's your lucky night."

Not yet being able to put emotions to the meaning in his words, Catherine took one more long look at him, and finally turned and walked to the front door. Before she got there, the car disappeared taking the men and the music with it into the night. Catherine looked back at the emptiness, the street light shining on nothing but parked cars and garbage cans. An airplane droned high overhead, and that was it. Surely one of the quietest neighborhoods in this giant city.

Catherine entered the silent house, but she felt her parents' alertness. It vibrated down the stairs even before the hall light went on. She understood that her mother and father had been only half-asleep, wondering why she had not yet returned.

Catherine lived on her own in Brooklyn, as she had for some time. It had been easier for her mother and father, at least simpler, since she was away from home most of the time. She was independent now, and they had learned to let go of being anxious about her life and habits. But, since Mateo's terrible accident, Catherine had been borrowing her parents' car to drive to the hospital in Amherst, and Joe and Bernadette Luna found they had quickly reverted to worrying about their daughter as they had when she was a teenager. On this night they had gone to bed and pretended to sleep, but in fact, neither had been able to do more than a light slumber. Through their fitful sleep they had heard the music from the car on the street, and at the faint sound of Catherine's key in the door, they both slid out of bed and went downstairs, turning lights on as they went, to see their daughter in the entry hall. Her back was to them and they saw her putting down her cello and backpack. Catherine was wearing, of all things, a huge black sweatshirt with a vivid Bob Marley portrait on the back.

"Catherine?" Bernie Luna sounded tentative.

"Baby, are you alright?" Her dad immediately knew something was wrong.

"I'm okay, Mom, Dad." At the sight of her parents, Catherine focused on calming them. Instead of dissolving into a frightened child, once she was standing in front of her doting parents in their night clothes, hair disarrayed, sleepy faces reflecting their worry, she only wanted to protect them.

"Don't worry." She said to no avail.

"What the hell's going on, Catherine?" Joe paced to and fro around his daughter, not sure what to do.

Bernie went up to Catherine and hugged her tightly. "Is it Mateo? Is he okay? You should have called us. We could have come up to be with you. Is his mother okay?" Bernie went on at some length until finally Catherine stopped her by putting her hand up.

"No, Mom, Mateo is the same. No better, no worse."

"Well, then, what is it? And what are you wearing? Have you been drinking?" Bernie smelled the alcohol on the sweatshirt, and the other smell she couldn't quite recognize. But Joe looked at his daughter carefully. He had not thought Catherine had time for such partying between her music and running back and forth to visit her injured boyfriend.

"Dad, it's the car. I wrecked your car. It's still out on the freeway because it was too banged up to drive. These guys gave me a ride home." She looked at the sweatshirt for the first time. "Oh damn, I didn't give Terrance his sweatshirt back. Looks like a new one, too."

She looked at her parents. Her eyes grew bigger and tears began to form. "I was so cold. I was shaking so much that he gave me his sweatshirt."

This time when her mother embraced her, Catherine melted into her and then began to cry softly. Bernie looked at Joe over their daughter's shoulder. "Let's run you a hot bath, honey." It was Bernie's cure-all for everything. Bernie led Catherine up the stairs and into the front bathroom with the old claw foot tub. Soon the water was running.

Joe stood there as if not sure what to do. Then he walked outside in his pajamas and looked all around to see for himself that his car was nowhere in sight. He looked up and down the street as if he could find where Catherine had come from, dropped out of the sky, it seemed. He came back in, put on his pants and shirt, and picked up his phone. Hearing the murmuring of Bernie and Catherine in the bathroom, he stood by the door and then knocked softly. Bernie poked her head out.

"Uh, Bernie, is Catherine okay? I mean, is she hurt, you know, in any way? Should we call the cops. . . ."

Bernie shook her head, understanding what he was unable to ask. "She says no. She's not hurt in any way. No one hurt her, and the accident didn't hurt her, either. I still am not sure what happened to the car, or where it is. But she is quite firm that no one hurt her, that she got a ride from the freeway with some guys."

Joe cleared his throat, some relief on his face. "So Bernie, find out where the car is, will ya? I'll go see if I can figure out what happened."

Bernie closed the door and he could hear the sound of their voices under the pouring spigots. When Bernie opened the door again a cloud of steam fogged up his glasses.

"She isn't sure, Joe. But she remembers passing that big Sporting Equipment store where we got the new bike for her. She said the accident must have been right before that because she remembers seeing that store right after she got in the car with . . ." and here Bernie gulped, " . . . with those men."

Joe nodded. He knew where it was then, an hour or more away with no traffic. It was still early enough in the morning to beat the morning rush. "I'll call you if I find out anything, Bernie." They exchanged one of those looks that long-married couples share when they have had a good life together. And he walked out the door to his pickup. Before leaving his neighborhood, he called his friend, Jay.

Jay was a highway patrol officer and used to being summoned at all hours. He sounded completely alert and awake when he answered Joe's call. By the time Joe drove to his house, he was up and dressed and both men climbed into his patrol car and headed out onto the freeway. Joe explained as much as he could, given how little he knew. Jay whistled as he heard the story. He alerted the highway patrol on duty and by the time he and Joe found the car, another patrol car was already there. As the traffic roared past him, Jay walked back to the overpass and inspected the scene.

Meanwhile, Joe walked around his car and with the help of Jay's flashlight and the headlights of the patrol car, he saw the right side of the Honda deeply scraped, like a giant razor had been taken from the front to the back of the car. The side mirror was gone, as was the protective strip that ran down the side of the doors. The back bumper was torn off. Liquid was leaking from beneath the car and the undercarriage clearly was damaged. Joe stared with horror at where his daughter had been traveling, his eyes looking back towards the freeway overpass. Being a city girl, how had his daughter, inexperienced as she was with driving, kept the car from flipping out of control after such a close encounter? He shuddered.

"She scraped the side of that overpass." Jay observed quietly, coming back to stand by his friend. "She's damn lucky, it looks like."

Joe was silent. His fist softly tapped on the car as he gazed back and forth between the car and the bridge. What had happened? He forced himself to remember that Catherine was safe at home with Bernie at that moment, no doubt being put to bed with a warm blanket and hot chocolate. She had said she was okay. But how could she be? And how did she come to be riding home with a car full of men at 3:00 in the morning? Joe's heart raced with protective zeal.

Jay watched his friend solicitously. Friends since grade school, he and Joe had shared plenty of wild adventures as young men before both settling down to lives of steady marriages and work. He knew Joe very well.

"Tow truck coming right up, Joe. Shall we have it towed to Al's Garage?"

Joe just grunted his affirmation, still unnerved by the situation.

"She's lucky," Jay repeated.

Joe rubbed his eyes, and for another fifteen minutes until the tow truck arrived, he said little. On the way home he thanked his friend for coming along and expediting the process. This time it was Jay who just nodded, but then finally added his question.

"So, you pretty sure Catherine is okay and nothing happened to her?"

Joe shrugged and slumped into his side of the patrol car. "I don't know much. But she was adamant. You know Catherine. She has a strong will, but she has always been a straight shooter. Never lied to us as far as I know. Sometimes tries to protect us, I can see that, but never lied. And she's been so worked up about Mateo, ya know, her boyfriend who got hurt real bad. She's stressed about him and about this big audition she is preparing for. Nerve-wracking, ya know. It's a famous string group, Tapestry is its name. She's so talented, my Catherine, but she's stressed about being good enough to make the cut for the group. She feels, ya know, like everyone is watching her. So yeah, I'm sure she is stressed. Real stressed," he repeated. And then added, "I don't want to think about what could have happened with a car full of men on the freeway at night, but that's all I can think about." He cleared his throat nosily. "But she says no one hurt her. I hope to hell she is telling the truth."

"Yeah, me too, Joe. For her sake and yours."

"And their sake," Joe added darkly.

Keeping his eyes on the road, Jay made his friend promise that if he found out that anyone had touched her that he would call Jay first before going off half-cocked and ready for a fight. "Besides," he added, "You don't even know who these guys were. It's a big city, my friend."

"Yeah, but I'm her daddy, and there isn't a city too big that a daddy can't find someone who hurts his girl."

Redirecting the dangerous tone in the conversation, Jay told his friend, "Listen, Joe, Catherine said nothing happened, so believe her, and, remember, she didn't hit that wall, she walked away, so focus on that!" Jay continued try to lighten the mood. "By the way, Joe, how did your girl get to be such a good musician? I've heard you at karaoke, and you can't sing to save your ass. Never saw Bernie do anything musical, either."

A chance to brag about his Catherine calmed Joe. "It was her grandpa, Bernie's dad, crusty old codger. He's a violinist, nothing too fancy, community bands, orchestras, you know. But he took Cate to a concert when she wasn't even in kindergarten yet. That's all she would talk about after that. He bought her a cello, a little kid-sized thing. I thought it was crazy, but she never got tired of it, she practiced all the time, even when her friends were hanging out at the mall and all that teenage stuff, she practiced. Lessons all the time."

Jay laughed, "That's why you worked all those extra hours."

"Yeah, that's my girl and I'd do anything for my girl."

The next morning Catherine found herself waking up in her old childhood bedroom. The brush with death came back to her in a rush, and her body reminded her as well, with a deep ache from her neck to her arms and her lower back. Catherine groaned when she thought of the private lesson she had to teach to a new student that morning, followed by cello rehearsal that afternoon. There had been a reason she had driven back from Mateo's hospital room in the middle of the night and then fallen asleep on the road in her exhausted state.

While she had welcomed the comfort of her mother's arms the night before, this morning Catherine regained her usual independent attitude. Painfully she pulled herself out of bed and found some clean clothes still remaining in her girlhood closet. She heard a faint snoring sound as she passed her parent's bedroom; it was Bernie, and Catherine didn't wake her.

Downstairs she made herself a cup of coffee and chewed on a day-old bagel she found in the bread box. Standing there in the kitchen she forced herself to think of the day ahead and nothing else. She was still there checking the bus schedule she kept in her purse and putting the last bite of bagel in her mouth, when Joe came to the kitchen door, dressed in his work clothes.

Father and daughter exchanged a long look.

"You headed out?"

"Uh-huh."

"Like a ride to the train?"

"Yes, sure, thanks, Daddy." Then, in a rush, "I'm really sorry about the car. I think it's pretty bad. I'll pay for it. May have to be in payments, but I'll pay for it. I'm so sorry."

"Cate. I don't care about the car. It's you. What happened? Can you tell me?"

Catherine looked down at the schedule, studying it intently for a second before taking a big breath and answering. "I fell asleep. Dad. I know you always tell me to pull off and take a nap if I get sleepy, but I didn't know I was sleepy until . . . I was dreaming, I guess . . . then suddenly I woke up because a car horn woke me up, but then I saw the wall . . . and, it was right in front of me . . . and . . ." Catherine was unable to go on.

Silence filled the kitchen. Joe finally nodded and walked past Catherine to the door, but as he did so he put his hand on her head and ruffled her hair as he had done when she was young. He let his hand rest there like a priest giving a blessing. Behind her, facing towards the door, he spoke gruffly.

"Catie, I'm just so relieved you're okay. You may think this is over with, but it isn't. You, me, your mom, we'll all keep going over this and over this, but you especially will relive this when you least expect it. I understand you wanting to just get on with your life. It's probably not a bad strategy, but be prepared when this comes back to grab you, baby. It will. Find some way to face those demons."

Catherine didn't speak but stayed there, wishing her father would never remove his warm hand from her head. Joe continued, "Can you give me this, Catie, can you tell me if you really are okay, ya know, with those men who brought you home? Do you know who they are? Where they come from? Are you really okay?"

"Daddy, I really am okay. I know it looks like it was a stupid thing to do, getting into their car - total strangers. I know all kinds of horrible things could have happened. I haven't let myself think about that yet - I'm just so lucky to be alive - but, nothing did happen. It was like I was in a dream. I know I should have tried to send them away and wait for a patrol car, or called you, but, well, my phone battery was dead anyway. The truth is I was just frozen because I was so scared, and then Terrance came along and I just went with him. He tried to warn me by honking his horn. And I'm sure he kept me safe. I'm sure of that. He drove me straight here. And, Daddy, I'm so sorry about the car."

"Damn it, Catherine, I don't care about the car."

Joe moved on to the door. "Ride?"

Catherine picked up her cello and backpack once again and followed her father to his pickup for the ride to her train. They didn't talk on the way. When Joe stopped by the curb for her to hop out, all he could say was, "Take care of yourself, pumpkin."

"Yeah, Daddy, I will. Thanks. Thanks for everything."

She turned and walked off, turning once to wave to him. She looked so young, Joe thought. How could he just let her go off on her own like this? But he did. He had to. It was so wickedly hard sometimes, he thought, as he contemplated Mateo's trauma and now Catherine's.

He was still thinking along those lines after he got to his office. He had no more walked into the door when Bernie called him wondering if he knew where their daughter was. Bernie had finally gotten to sleep just before dawn, after sitting by Catherine's bed for hours.

"Calling in sick today," she told Joe. "I'm simply exhausted, and then later I'm going down to church to light a candle of gratitude for Catherine's good fortune."

"Her good fortune?" Joe sounded skeptical. "I'd hardly call it that. What a nightmare, is what I call it."

"Oh, no, Joe, dear heart. Catherine missed a horrible collision last night. She had an angel watching her all night long, to warn her and bring her home, and an angel of quite unlikely description from what Catherine told me."

Joe stared at the 2005 calendar on his wall. Joseph Luna Construction Company. He had done well for himself, given his beginnings. Even Bernie's father had come around eventually. It had been hard at first. Bernadette's father had seen Joe Luna as a feckless young man, up to little good, lacking ambition and future. Bernie had always believed in him, though, and she had defied her father and married Joe. For three years there had been no visiting, no family events, nothing. Then when Catherine was born, Bernie's mom pulled rank and told her husband that the war was over. Bernie and Joe and Catherine were family and they would be treated like family. But it was Bernie's ever-positive spirit and belief that had made Joe reach inside and do the best he could do. He found that the man inside him was a pretty good man indeed.

When friends asked him what Catherine's boyfriend did and wondered whether Joe liked Mateo, he found that he could honestly reply yes. He saw that Mateo was underachieving. Mateo came from an educated family, but he worked as a barista; twenty-eight-years-old and working in a coffee shop, for God's sake. A good enough job to work your way through college, but surely not enough.

"Not enough for what?" His intuitive wife would ask with a twinkle in her eye. "Not enough to be with your daughter? Not enough to fit into your world?"

And, fair man that he was, protective father or no, Joe had to admit that Mateo was as good a man at age twenty-eight as he himself had been, and indeed probably a fair bit more stable than Joe had been. And he also had to admit that like Mateo, he lacked a college degree, unlike Bernadette and Catherine, and it did not make them unworthy men.

Now, though, everything hung in limbo. Mateo's and Catherine's lives had taken a horrendous turn three weeks earlier. On a visit back to his Massachusetts home town, Mateo Schumacher had been attacked by an angry young man who, in a case of truth being stranger than fiction, turned out to be Mateo's unknown cousin. The assault had put Mateo in a coma and now he floated somewhere between life and death.

Joe jerked himself back to listen to Bernie's effusive emotions regarding their daughter's narrow escape. Bernie had a simple faith in people despite the grim reality she saw day in and day out at the hospital. This probably made her the good nurse she was. And to her it seemed quite plausible that a man of questionable lifestyle, bearing only the name Terrance, could materialize in the middle of the night to take care of their daughter. Joe shook his head at his wife's naiveté and yet loved her for it.

Catherine had nightmares about the car accident, nightmares where she was back on that jolting horse and facing the concrete wall. This happened often enough for her to realize that a trauma of this magnitude had changed her. Sometimes she thought it helped her to empathize more with Mateo. She found that her music helped her deal with the emotions even more than talking about it, although she did seek out a few listening ears.

Not Mateo's ears, though. Not for a very long time after he regained consciousness and struggled through rehabilitation therapy. It was two years later that she finally told him what happened that night. She didn't want to. She didn't want him to feel responsible, to burden him with her trauma. Since she had not been harmed, she wondered why she could not just shake off the memory or laugh about it. But she could not forget her terror. It was from that terror that she wanted to protect Mateo. When she finally did tell him, it was actually a relief. The worst part was dwelling on what didn't happen, what almost happened, what could have happened, for both of them. But they had survived. They always came back to that.

After Catherine's accident, Joe and Bernie went on being companions in life and love in a quiet, satisfying way. But a few days after the accident, "that night" as they called it, Bernie brought out the sweat shirt that Catherine had worn home that night. While the presence of Terrance on the night of the accident had been powerful for Catherine, she did not seem to give the man much thought afterward. It was perhaps self-preservation that required that she not dwell on the details of that night, even about the man who had helped and protected her.

The same was not true for Bernie and Joe. It was such a mystery - the car and the men - although without the presence of the sweatshirt, they could perhaps have let that piece of the incident pass from their memories. But the sweatshirt that laid on the coffee table pulsed like a voice for someone, something. Something decent and good. A stranger, yet a man who had had the potential to alter the Luna family's life forever, for tragedy or for good. An angel, Bernie believed. A decent man, Joe thought, out there in this big city somewhere. Bernie was able to assign this mysterious Terrance to a place among the saints to whom she gave thanks and homage. And she prayed for Terrance, this unknown man, every night for the rest of her life, silently, without telling Joe, who knew she did this without letting on he knew.

But for Joe, it was different. He possessed a strong sense of justice and acknowledgement, so it was difficult for him to just put this event behind him as he guessed Catherine had done, considering it a chance encounter in the big city with a good outcome. Nor could he give it over to God as his wife did, being sure that all would come out beautifully in some karmic future. Joe was of a different mindset, and while he kept his own counsel, he stewed on this issue for a month.

Then, in typical Joe fashion, he began acting. Although he lived in the suburbs now, he was born and raised in the lower East Side. He knew the City pretty well, and from the few comments he could get from Catherine about the men and the circumstances of that night, he narrowed down some areas of town he thought he might be most successful in his search. One evening a week, on Thursdays, when Bernie was at her book group, he bundled up the sweatshirt in a bag and started his quest, from one neighborhood to another, from one bar-room to another, from one street corner to another. In the course of two years, he was mugged once (but not for the sweatshirt, only his wallet, which relieved him, but distressed Bernie), drank a lot of both bad and very good beer and whiskey and coffee, and was often solicited by disappointed pimps and prostitutes thinking he was a john on the lookout in a neighborhood not his own. He overheard a great deal of street culture he had not imagined, well beyond his own rambling youth in his Italian neighborhood. Joe was changed in ways he had never expected that had little to do with a man named Terrance.

It didn't occur to Joe to give up. It became the pattern in his week, part of his schedule around work, construction inspections, Saturday dates with his wife, Monday night poker at Jay's house, and Sunday dinners in his own mother's kitchen where the Italian food and energy was breathed in like a fresh breeze on a hot day. He never told even Bernie what he was up to on his weekly excursions. She knew in some way that he was on a mission, but she also knew it was his own private quest, his own exercise in gratitude for his daughter's life and safety. And in time it became bigger than that. It became his own dive into greater understanding of the City where he had been born and raised.

Two years. Every Thursday evening. Despite a few unsavory encounters, for the most part Joe was ignored. He most enjoyed watching the children in the neighborhoods, both their innocence and their bravado. He found himself wondering about their school life and home life, their opportunities and future challenges. He felt connected to the flavor of each neighborhood he got to know. It was a big city and all sorts of people walked the streets.

One evening, just as he was thinking it was time to find the subway home, Joe made his way out of a bar and onto the street. He passed a group sitting and standing around a man playing steel drums. The cannabis smoke was thick, and the singing and laughing voices were loud. Joe walked by, working his way into the street to pass. Then he heard someone call out the name, "Terrance." Joe froze. How many Terrances lived in New York City? Over the last two years, he had discovered several men of that name, but none had been the correct one.

Wondering if he should nose his way into this group, whether it would be prudent or not, he saw the car. Sitting there as big as life, an old silver Lincoln Continental with kamikaze doors, just as Catherine had remembered. It was one of the few things she had noticed that night.

Joe found his heart pounding. A bit of fear, and a lot of excitement. Without giving himself a chance to analyze the safety of what he was about to do, he walked to the circle of men and almost pushed his way through.

An annoyed explosion of arms and words came at him from those he had pushed aside. But he pressed on until he was in front of the man playing the drums. The man looked like he was in a trance, but Joe didn't care, he shouted loudly, standing right in front of the strong-looking man with the long dreadlocks and half-shut eyes.

"Terrance? Terrance? Are you Terrance?"

It took at least ten times for Joe to shout the name before the man opened his eyes and focused on Joe. There was a tension in the crowd but no one moved, waiting to see what Terrance might do.

"Who wants to know?"

Joe didn't answer with words. Feeling strangely calm and confident, he simply took out the sweatshirt and handed it to the man with the drumming mallets in his hands. For a long time there was a standoff: Joe holding the sweatshirt and Terrance eyeing him with distrust, masking his confusion. But Joe did not back off. Just stood there.

"I think this is yours."

Putting down the pan mallet sticks, Terrance reached out and took the shirt in his impossibly large hands. His brown eyes, liquid with the effect of his smoking, looked straight into Joe's face, and he saw nothing to fear from this sixty-year-old Italian man from a different part of town.

As the sweatshirt fell open in his hands and he looked at it, a slow glimmering of remembrance came over his face, and, with it, a grin. And he had a beautiful smile, Joe noted.

"Hey, say, that crazy chick with the big fiddle. Almost smashed herself on the highway. Long time ago."

"I've been looking for you. I wanted to thank you for helping my little girl, well, my daughter that night. And I wanted to return your sweatshirt."

Joe held out his hand to shake, and after a moment and a big laugh, Terrance reached out a hand that dwarfed Joe's own capable hand. For that brief second, Joe felt something relax and he knew he had satisfied a deep need.

Joe turned to go, not knowing what else there was to say or do, but Terrance called after him. "Hey, how's she doing? Still playing that cello?"

Joe smiled at him, and for a moment it was only Terrance and Joe on the street. "Yeah, she is. She's doing real, real, good, too."

"Some gutsy girl she was. Couldn't get over how she steered around that fucking cement wall. And then all she cared about was that her cello was okay. Gotta love that. Being a musician myself, ya know. But glad we got out of your neighborhood alive, though. My brothers were not happy we went there. But she's good, so that's good."

Joe reached into his pocket and pulled out his business card. "If you know of anyone who might want a job. I do hire from time to time."

Terrance gave a laugh but he took the card and tucked it into his own pocket of his sagging pants.

This time Joe did walk away, and as Terrance called after him, "Hey, thanks, man, for my sweatshirt. It was a new one, and it's my man Marley."

Joe waved over his shoulder and moved on home. He arrived safely and slept well that night.

Six months later Joe walked into his office and found his office manager nervously trying to usher a young man out of the office. He looked at her flustered face and asked what was up.

"This person says he is looking for a job. I told him we have no job opening and that you were out and couldn't be bothered."

Joe looked at the young man, a boy really, impossibly young and defiant and nervous and scared behind his bravado. As Joe looked at him, the boy drew out a torn and smudged business card, Joe's, and, deliberately looking out the window while he was talking to Joe, he mumbled, "Said you might give me a job."

Joe opened his office door and told him to come inside. He calmed his loyal manager before closing the door behind him.

"Tell me who you are and how you happen to have my card."

Again the boy stared away while answering.

"My brother said you would give me a job, maybe anyway."

"And your brother is . . . ?"

The boy looked at Joe briefly as if Joe had said something very stupid. "Terrance."

"Ah!" Joe looked at the boy through different eyes now but found little in the fellow in front of him to remind him of the impressively tall man who sat behind the steel drums with clouds of marijuana floating around him. Could this be the brother of the owner of the extra large black sweatshirt that had sheltered his daughter from more than the cold that night?

"How's Terrance doing?"

The boy muffled his answer and Joe could barely understand, but managed to catch the unfortunate news. "Prison. . . awhile. Told me to get a job and not end up in prison. Gave me your card. Made me come. So I'm here."

There was a silence in the room. Joe moved to the water cooler and got a cup of water and gave it to the boy who took it and kept looking at the floor across the room with an attitude that said he didn't care one way or another, but yet, he was here against all likelihood. Joe marveled again at the amazing sway that Terrance held over people.

"Your name?"

"Roger."

"Do you have a last name?"

"Parsons."

"Well, Roger, it just so happens that I'm looking for a new apprentice. Doesn't pay much at first, but that could change over time. I do have one beginning requirement, however."

Roger looked up at Joe with attention masked by attitude, but Joe kept talking, ignoring the young man's discomfort. "Yes, I have one requirement for my workers. And that is that you show up, every work day, on time. Nothing else matters in the beginning. I'll teach you as much as you can learn. Whether that is a lot or a little is up to you. Just in the beginning, you must show up. No excuses. You do what it takes to make that happen, got it? Show up tomorrow morning wearing clothes that you can work in. If you don't have any, I can get you some, and if you like you can change here at work if you don't want to wear them home."

The young man was unsure how to be cool and be grateful at the same time, so he said nothing.

Joe just waved his arm in dismissal. "Just show up, 8:00 tomorrow morning. That's your first assignment. Then we'll talk about pay and work."

When Roger didn't respond, Joe said very directly, "Got it?"

"Yeah, uh, yes."

"Okay, and Roger, you probably didn't want to come down here and ask for a job, did you? Terrance probably made you, right?" Roger did not deny this, but said nothing. "Well, I don't know what Terrance did to be sent to prison, but I know something about him. He was a good man to my daughter, and he's a good man to his brother. You know that?"

Roger nodded, the first sign of softness appearing on his face. "I'll be here tomorrow, Mr. Joe."

Joe watched the door shut behind the young man, Terrance's brother, and wondered realistically whether this would work out. Bernie would believe it could and would. He was more pragmatic and wondered what he was getting himself into. But he felt he owed it to Terrance, to Catherine, even to his city, and perhaps most importantly to himself, to give Roger Parsons a fair chance. And when Joe put his mind to anything, he had never been a man to give up midstream.

12

MUSIC & MYSTERIES

Vic & Cecilia

2005

Vic and Cecilia dropped into their center seats, front row of the balcony, Cecilia's favorite seats in any theater or concert hall, up high with a view but still in the middle of the action. For the joy of her company, Vic gladly passed on his own favorite seats, front and center in the lower section where he felt the best acoustics could be found.

It had been an exhausting year for Cecilia's family. When Mateo, her son, was hospitalized in a coma after a head injury in late spring, his well-being had become the only thing that mattered. The small town of Pine Junction had all hurt together for the family and one of their favorite sons. And when, after three weeks, he had regained consciousness with his functioning relatively intact, a great cloud of relief could almost be seen above the trees of the town. Now with weeks of Mateo's rehabilitation behind them, Cecilia could see that her son was faring well in his brother Rowan's hands, and so she had agreed to leave Pine Junction for Amherst to hear this concert of the Hayden Mass. Vic and Cecilia were both musicians, she an amateur, and he an accomplished professional, and they eagerly anticipated the opportunity to revive themselves in fine music after months of being immersed in family dynamics and medical issues.

In a sense, it was their first official date. Cecilia was the town librarian and soprano in the church choir, and Vic was organist and choir director. For over twenty-eight years Vic had loved her silently while maintaining their friendship pure. It was a long time to hold a torch, but his monk-like patience was rewarded during the tumultuous spring of 2005, when they finally discovered each other as lovers. Here this night, months later, they laughed about having a first date after so many years. Both felt an anticipatory excitement.

The orchestra tuned and played warm-ups with that lovely pre-concert buzz. Cecilia felt almost normal, almost like she used to feel before her mother's death and Mateo's injuries, before all the secrets had exploded from her parents' past and her own, too. In fact, life was not simply back to normal, but far better now, as if a new life was dawning for her. At this moment she was fully present to the stage where the choir members in shimmering black moved elegantly into place. Having seen Cecilia's emotions overflowing on so many occasions recently, and knowing the potential evocative power of this Hayden work, Vic handed Cecilia a impeccably laundered white handkerchief. Cecilia took it and inspected it carefully.

"Victor Dalloway, this is beautiful - monogrammed and pressed!"

"Yes, I occasionally do laundry, Ceci. You know I don't live in the choir room, despite rumors to the contrary."

Cecilia smiled at this. Even as close as she had been to Vic all these years, what she learned in the last months since they had become lovers had enlightened her, and one was Vic's wonderful sense of humor.

Vic continued, "My mother always told me to have a clean handkerchief in my pocket."

"You know, that is the first gentle thing you have ever said about your mother, Vic."

Vic stared at the handkerchief as if it held a mystery for him. Almost reluctantly he said, "It's possible that I haven't given my mother a completely fair assessment over the years." He paused. "Lillian was her name."

"That's a beautiful name. You told me that she saved all your recital programs, that you found a whole draw full of programs after she died."

"She never showed up. She never stood up for me. She was a coward."

His pronouncements were matter-of-fact, but Cecilia noted the childish pain underlying his accusations.

"I know it's hard to get past that. I get it, Vic. That must have really hurt you." She thought of her own parents and their faithful attendance at each and all events where their three daughters had a part. Of course she had taken it for granted. Now she sympathized with Vic. "That's a real omission in your life, your family life."

". . . there were commissions, too." Decades later Vic still winced to remember the harsh words, the whistle of the belt descending.

Cecilia gave a sigh.

"I'm so sorry, Vic. Still, it's nice to hear you have some little detail about your mother that is tender, or at least neutral, even if it is something as insignificant as a handkerchief."

Cecilia thought a moment and continued. "And maybe the handkerchief was a way to try to care about you. I mean, Vic, it's something."

"I suppose. " Vic wasn't going to argue with Cecilia on such an evening.

"Now, I'm waiting to hear one good thing about your father."

She spoke playfully, but was immediately sorry she had spoken, as Vic scowled. "Don't push it, Ceci. You'll have to wait forever for that to happen."

Cecilia squeezed Vic's arm while she reassured him that she had no intention of pushing further on this splendid night.

The lights dimmed on the audience. Vic gazed ahead at the choir, but for a few minutes his mind was thinking in a new way. He contemplated the long-held secrets in Cecilia's family that had recently overflowed almost simultaneously into trauma, the worst being Mateo's coma. Thankfully Mateo was making a good recovery now; he was a young man very dear to Vic's heart. But through all these occurrences, including Cecilia's mother's death, ordinary life had been suspended for everyone in the family. Vic had become Cecilia's lover and devoted friend, but still, technically, a bystander. He admitted now that it was easy to play that role. Easier to help someone else, someone you love, come to terms with her family skeletons. Hand the handkerchief to someone else. That he could do.

But how about his own family? Vic had never given his Canadian family members even the benefit of a possibility that they, too, may have had painful histories that had limited their lives. But something must have accounted for the lack of kindness and connection among the members of the small Dalloway family. He pictured his mother, Lillian. Slender, faded and fragile, detached, ghostly - those were the adjectives that came first to his mind. In his current state of happiness, Vic could afford to be more expansive in his thinking - Lillian Dalloway had not sprung forth from the womb with those haunting attributes. Life had happened, and she had interacted with life in such a way as to make her the woman who raised him, and, he felt, abandoned him. Vic swallowed hard and stared at the concert program without reading it.

As for his father, he could not, even at this point, bear to imagine what had turned his father into a brute of a man - cruel, angry, unhappy, unrelenting, bullheaded - the list of describing words always went like that. But, and Vic hesitated to think about this, how had that come about? How had Robert Dalloway, a successful businessman, become such a vicious man, and what might have been going on under the surface? What unknown circumstances made him become the man from whom his son, Vic - artistic, certainly overly sensitive, but perhaps just as stubborn - had run? Vic moved uncomfortably in his seat. Had he escaped from his parents, or had he abandoned them just as they had abandoned him? Both had died years earlier, but Vic had already left Canada for good by then, so it was a moot point. Or was it?

Cecilia folded her program, ready to listen. She had never heard this Hayden piece performed live before, but it was one of her favorites. She whispered to Vic with a twinkle in her eyes.

"Vic, let me know if you need to share the hankie."

Vic's eyes lost their strained look and sent warmth back at her. He said nothing, but indicated his pocket where another linen handkerchief poked out, the initial "L" for Lillian, visible to those who knew to look.

The lights in the hall dimmed to darkness, and the stage glowed with a soft light. The audience grew silent as they awaited the arrival of the conductor on stage, and Vic quickly brought himself back to the present with a rush of happiness that he was sitting with Ceci, ready to get caught up in the music.

Cecilia slipped something into his pocket.

"What's that?"

She whispered back to him. "Just a little poem I wrote for you last night when I couldn't sleep. You can read it later."

Before Vic could take a peek at the paper or even thank her, the conductor walked out on stage and Vic and Cecilia were soon transformed, all pain and worries and past stupidities forgotten in the perfection of the music. The world's suffering and joy, including their own, was flushed out by voice and instrument. It was a universal acknowledgement of aches and agonies as well as the expression of pure beauty.

Vic thought of the vital parts of life: relationship, love, art, nature, music, even science. What underlay all of these? Yearnings, he thought. To weep, to soar, to imagine, to create. To love and to be beloved. He thought of Cecilia and touched the poem in his pocket. His mind probed this thought. We crave beauty in our lives. Is it divine beauty or human beauty, or perhaps the intersection of humanity and divinity? What is divine? What does that mean?

Now, with the first notes, his throat tightened and then relaxed completely. It was the essential longing in the music that brought him tears and yet gave him soul-satisfying pleasure. As for the mysteries, it was not about words, anyway. Not tonight. His mind became calm. Tomorrow the mysteries of life would once again invite pursuing through philosophical inquiry or theological language. But not tonight. Tonight was the experience of the beauty itself. Vic reached for Cecilia's hand, knowing that tomorrow held the promise of a poem . . . and the poet.

To Vic from Cecilia

Time passed, days, years
When the time was right, I washed up on
    your shore
Pressed my body against the firm but pliant
    sand
Felt the heat of the sun and the cold bite of
    the sea
The waves crashed on rock and beach
Climax of a four thousand mile journey

The heartbeat of the surf throbbed in me
I lay my face on the grains of a million pul-
    verized stones
A new resting spot for me
A sanctuary

When I needed someone to talk to
You answered me

And now we sit in silence together on our
    shore

13

THE HEFT OF A FEW WORDS

Cecilia & Warren

2008

It was a cold January day, the first day of the Western Massachusetts Librarians Symposium, and Cecilia was in a funk as she drove towards Amherst. This conference was traditionally one of the highlights of her year, but this year the conference was off to a strange start. The weekend snow storm that had closed down much of the region had not hit the Amherst area dramatically, so her roads were open. But two of Cecilia's close colleagues from further afield were unable to get out of their driveways. Cecilia had received their early morning emails with a sinking heart. Her entire alumni group was now a no-show, because, in addition, for the first year, she would miss two other librarian friends who had retired. However, the last straw this morning was a phone call Cecilia had received just as she was heading out the door. Gina, a new librarian friend from Amherst, was dreadfully sick with a stomach bug and would have to stay home today. "Maybe tomorrow," Gina said, before a quick goodbye as she dropped her phone and headed for the bathroom again.

Cecilia had not realized how much of her enjoyment of the conference came from her friendships with these other librarians, especially the four she had known since graduate school. Why would anyone want to retire, Cecilia grumbled to herself, although she knew that her friends' retirements had been prompted more by their husbands' desires than their own. She wondered if she would retire and move away if that were Vic's dream. Well, perhaps, but she could not imagine either she or Vic retiring from the work they loved so much: Vic a musician and organist, and she a small town librarian. To her, their life together was very nearly perfect, both at work and at home.

As she approached Amherst, Cecilia gave herself a pep talk, promising to focus on the workshops and speakers. The conference, after all, had always provided good stimulation, above and beyond the delight of spending two days with colleagues and friends she didn't see often enough. For the most part that morning, she found her two workshops informative, but, in her strange mood, she did not mix with other attendees, merely saying a general hello to those who called out to her as she passed.

By noon, Cecilia was still not inclined to join anyone else for lunch, so she slipped out into the white world letting the winter chill bite her cheeks and revive her. Bundled in her heaviest coat, scarf, and knit hat, she walked down the street to a cafe. She hung her coat on the hooks in the lobby and left her snow boots there too, walking into the cafe in her flats.

Finding a corner table, Cecilia sat down, ordered some soup and bread, and opened her book. Over the years she had lived alone, she spent many a meal with a good book, and always found her literary friends to be excellent company. After about forty-five minutes, she paid her check, stuffed her paperback into her bag and pushed her chair back. But as she did so, she looked across the busy cafe and saw Warren Schumacher sitting in the opposite corner, looking squarely at her.

Her ex-husband looked much the same as he had over thirty years ago when she first laid eyes on him: tall, lean, with handsome facial features dominated by his unusual gray eyes, which were both distant and inviting at the same time. His fair hair, beginning to gray and kept close-cropped, had gradually receded, but did not detract from his striking good looks.

Having made eye contact, Cecilia had no choice but to go say hello. In the last seventeen years since their divorce, she saw Warren only occasionally. Of course, he had come around when Mateo was in the hospital three years ago in 2005, and, later that same year, Warren had attended her mother Victoria's memorial service, although he had slipped quickly away on that occasion and Cecilia had only glimpsed his retreating figure.

As Cecilia walked the fifteen feet toward his table, Warren watched her approach. He noticed that she had gained a little weight, and that her hair was still thick, shoulder-length with gray showing in more abundance now: clearly, she had not been interested in coloring her hair. As usual, Cecilia dressed elegantly, but also casually, and slightly unconventionally. Today she had on a long dark-blue tunic-like shirt over a mid-calf-length skirt of various shades of blue and black and gray. She wore black tights and ballerina-style shoes, and over her tunic she had a turquoise short vest and a royal-blue scarf wrapped around her neck. Her earrings flashed and swung as she walked; perhaps they were abalone, he thought. It was not his taste, and not his current wife's style, but, somehow, it worked on Cecilia. Nearly sixty, she looked striking, an interesting term given that it was exactly the word Cecilia had mentally used in her quick assessment of him.

He looked at her and he approved. He looked at her and he disapproved. That was the way it had always been between them. With Tanya, his second wife, he always approved. But, he had to admit, he was still excited seeing Cecilia walk towards him. That, also, was always the way it had been.

"Hi, Warren."

"Hi, Cecilia. What brings you to Amherst in the middle of the week?"

"Annual Library Conference. I come every year."

"All by yourself?"

"With retirements, road conditions, and bad health, I find myself without my old friends, and I was just in the mood for a solitary lunch, I guess." She wasn't sure why she was explaining so much. "How's Tanya? And Sarah?" Sarah was Warren's step-daughter.

"Fine. Tanya's art gallery is holding its own. And Sarah's enjoying a study year abroad in Spain. She'll graduate next spring."

"Spain is a wonderful place to study and travel." In reality, Cecilia and Vic rarely traveled, although they felt that they traveled wherever their books and music took them.

"Yes, she's having a blast. "

There was a silence. And then, as if remembering his manners, Warren asked. "How's Vic doing? Still playing the organ in Pine Junction?"

Somehow, to her ears, Warren made it sound vaguely pathetic and Cecilia bristled.

"Yes. He gave a concert recently that was sold out and received a rave review in the Amherst paper's Arts section."

Warren quickly replied, "I guess I missed it. Tanya usually grabs that section before I can even get my hands on it. Vic's a fine organist, that's for sure."

Cecilia and Warren looked at each other. She supposed she should comment about their sons, Rowan and Mateo, but, really, what was there to say? She didn't know exactly how often the two saw Warren, but she knew that they kept him updated about their lives. So Cecilia looked at her watch and moved a step backwards.

"It's good to see you, Warren. I better get back to the Conference."

"Sure. Hope you enjoy the rest of the day. Oh, how is your father doing?"

She stopped, half-turned to answer. "Papa is getting weaker all the time. Still able to do some things but we can see the effect of the Parkinson's becoming more pronounced. Thanks for asking."

"Rowan mentioned his decline a few weeks ago when he and I went to a Celtics game. Well, give Pedro my best."

Cecilia nodded and walked to the door of the cafe where several people were entering, stomping their feet and wiping their red noses. Warren opened the laptop on the table in front of him. He had come to the cafe to work because of some noisy construction at his office that morning. His mind was more jumbled by seeing Cecilia than he wanted to admit, and he looked back up to the door. There she was, coming straight back toward him, boots clomping and spreading splashes of melted snow, her coat half-on and half-off, her face looking purposeful. He was a little unnerved.

Cecilia pulled out the chair and sat down across from him. And without preamble she burst out softly, so softly that he leaned closer to hear, "I'm way overdue to say I'm sorry, Warren, but I hope you can accept my apologies after all these years."

Whatever Warren was expecting her to say or do, it was not this. So he sat there just looking at his ex-wife with his mouth half-open. For once, the ever-composed Warren Schumacher was discomposed.

Finally he answered, "I'm not sure what you're talking about, Cecilia."

"I'm sure you do know what I'm talking about, Warren."

He sat and looked at her. "Well, it was all a long time ago."

"Yes, but it has affected our whole life."

"All I can remember are the terrible things I yelled at you that day." Warren was surprised when this came out of his mouth, but then he added. "I was way out of line and said some vile things to you. It's my job to apologize to you, Cecilia."

Cecilia brushed away his words. "I appreciate that acknowledgement, although I was so unnerved that day that I spoke horribly to you, too. But no, that day, as traumatic as it was, isn't what I'm talking about."

He looked at her, flummoxed that they were even talking about the old times after all these years, and yet curious as to what else she might be referring to.

"Warren, how can you not hate me for the way I let us get married when I knew it wasn't the right thing to do, not even to give Mateo a father?"

Warren stared at her, but then quietly stated, "It was me who pushed you into it, Cecilia. I know that, and you must know that."

Cecilia shook her head emphatically. "I could have said no, but I was scared. I know that now. So I let you talk me into getting married."

Another big breath before she went on. "But then I didn't give you a fair shake after we made that commitment to each other. I moved away from you, you know . . . emotionally. I just didn't know how to relate to you. You were always so remote, and I was . . ." She left the thought hanging. "So I didn't try as much as I should. I just stayed enmeshed in the boys and my work. That wasn't fair to you."

She took a deep breath, then kept going: "And, of course, even before that . . . it was me who slept with Dane when you and I were engaged." Words never said aloud took on huge significance; oh, the heft of a few words! "I deceived him, too. He never knew I was engaged. He never knew I was pregnant. I thought it was a harmless and enjoyable fling at the time, but, Warren, it was wrong. There were other things I could have done, from saying no to him, to breaking up with you when I knew in my heart that we were not right for each other, not for the long run, no matter how attractive I found you. We were opposites, and, clearly, sometimes that just doesn't work."

Warren's eyes were blurring. He had no clue what to say to her. He was silent a long time, so long that Cecilia finally stood up to go.

She stood beside the table for a moment. "You don't have to answer me, Warren. I know I've shocked you and probably brought up issues that you've long put behind you. We've both gone on with our lives, although it sure took me a long time. It seems we are both content now. I don't want to disturb you."

She laughed. "I've surprised myself. I sure didn't get up this morning and think, 'Today I'll finally give Warren my apologies for my youthful misjudgments and the pain I caused him.' It just came from this unexpected opportunity, I suppose."

She thought for a moment, and then added. "But you know what? I'm glad the opportunity presented itself because it's healing for me to accept my share of the blame, to not just blame you. It wasn't just you, Warren. I hope you can accept my attempt to say I'm sorry for how I failed you, and us."

Another pause, "And Mateo."

Silence, then whispered."And Dane, too."

He nodded. Cleared his throat and closed his laptop and then opened it again and then closed it, finally. He nodded again. Cecilia gently laid her hand on his arm for a second. It was not flirtatious, just kind.

"I hope I'll see you at Mateo and Catherine's wedding, whenever they finally set a date." She smiled calmly. But it was different. All her life, Cecilia had appeared unruffled, but now, instead of a distanced calm, she felt truly present.

"Yes, sure, I'll be there." Warren had a great need to clear his throat, once, twice, again. "And Cecilia, let me know how it goes with Pedro, you know, how his health holds out, and if . . . ." He stopped awkwardly.

She finished his thought. "Sure, I'll let you know when he passes. We know it will come someday soon, and Papa knows it as well."

This time she did move to the door, putting her coat on as she walked away, and only looking forward.

Warren managed to call after her, "Cecilia. Thanks." But he was not sure whether she heard him. He was not entirely sure he had said it out loud.

14

JOURNEYS BEYOND

Rex

2013

Vanessa Jefferson groaned and pushed herself away from her computer, then stretched her arms and rolled her neck to get the cricks out. She was pure weary. This was absolutely the last piece of freelance editing work she was going to do, she swore once again. How many times had she made that bold statement, only to accept yet one more job when it came calling? Years of living on the financial edge as a single mother left her almost incapable of turning down work when it came knocking at her door, and, to be honest, she relished that she was still in demand, and hung on to each new contract like a lifeline. But now, at age sixty-five, she felt so tired of using her trained eyes to spot typos and commas that she wanted to scream. Creative revision work was one thing, but strictly being a copy editor was making her eyes cross these days. Someday, she thought for the thousandth time, I'll write my own book and then I won't mind being a proofreader. But for now, she was tired of it all.

Perhaps she could blame Rex for this relaxing of her professional intensity. Perhaps she could blame happiness for taking away her competitive drive, her compulsive need to keep working, never stopping, as if she could keep the fear of not being needed at bay. Thinking of Rex made her relax from head to toe, and, after stretching, she walked out of the former living room of her new home, a room she had turned into her office. Twelve months ago, she and Rex Randall had exchanged simple vows in front of a doting group of friends, family and parishioners, all of whom shared the couple's own happy surprise at this unlikely marriage.

Vanessa Jefferson was an editor, a long-divorced mother of three (her life-resume went on: Scrabble champion, lay minister, spirit-sister to a powerful group of community women, neighborhood activist, soft ball pitcher . . .). Sometimes she still could not believe that she was married to a recently-retired small-town pastor and living in this tiny, woodsy township, miles from Boston and her long urban life. And not only had she made this shift when she and Rex married, but after three-hundred-sixty-five days of this life, she was still walking in the clouds, all the while feeling as grounded and content as ever in her life.

They had given Pine Junction three-hundred-sixty-five days. That was the length of time she and Rex had decided to try it, to determine how their life together would work in the small town. And this was the anniversary of the day they came home from their honeymoon, spent near her late grandparent's home in Jamaica. The time - these three-hundred-sixty-five days - had passed so swiftly and pleasantly that her doubting friends had been left sheepishly dumbfounded by the newly contented Ms. Jefferson-Randall.

Vanessa walked into the library of the little house in the woods, now Rex's only office since his retirement as minister of the First Congregational Church. He had moved his books and other mementos of a lifetime of pastoral work out of the church offices and into his home, which he now shared with Vanessa. Rex at this moment was surrounded by stacks of books, and appeared to be deeply engrossed in one open on his lap. When his wife slid open the pocket doors, he looked up at her with delight, as if he could still not believe that he shared his life with such a beautiful, dynamic force. As it was with Vanessa, Rex kept pinching himself to see if this new life was real. After a year, he was starting to know it for certain. And it made him smile from the inside out.

"Through work for the day?"

"Cannot sit one more minute fixing spelling and hyphens and spacing errors!!"

"You're a wonder. But, you don't have to work so hard now, Vanessa."

"Maybe this will be the last job I take." But Vanessa grinned ruefully. "I'm my own worst enemy sometimes. And who are you to talk? You worked until you were my age, and more, yourself."

"Well, you've got me there. You're a spring chicken compared to me."

Rex put his book away and looked around the room. "I'm almost finished going through my library, and I'm surprised at how many books I'm ready to let go. I thought it would be hard to part with these old friends, but, in fact, I'm feeling like it is time to move many of them on. At least two-thirds of them I'll donate to the seminary library and then some more to Cecilia for the Pine Junction library, or the high school library, so that'll leave a very manageable-sized library to stay with me."

He got a faraway look in his eyes. "Once I preached a sermon about the 'bag ladies' of the retirement homes, how all their material goods in time were reduced to what they could carry in front of them in the bag on their walker. Well, I suppose we're all moving in that direction from the day we are born. I've been doing a lot of thinking, Vanessa, and when I look back on my life and work, I wonder if I've led a very small life. I wonder if I should've pushed harder to make more of a difference, to have accomplished more of significance, to have changed the world more profoundly. I sometimes wonder . . . have I let my life be too small?"

Vanessa's notorious verve leapt out of her in a flash. "Don't you go saying anything like that or thinking that kind of trash, Rex. I can tell you that, after waiting thirty years, I didn't marry any small man. You got that? There's nothing small about your life, Reverend Randall, nothing but power in that mind of yours and goodness in your heart! Just because no one made a statue of you, doesn't mean there shouldn't be one somewhere! Don't let me hear you having any regrets on your life, mister, or you'll have me to contend with!"

She came over to Rex, wrapped her arms around him, and nuzzling his cheek with her mouth, she whispered to him, "That day you bumped into me and spilled coffee all over my new dress was the luckiest day of my life, Reverend Rex."

Rex thankfully returned her embrace and they held each other for awhile, Vanessa closing her eyes and resting her tiredness against his chest, and Rex looking over her head out the window to the woods and snowy banks around his little house. He felt calm again. It had only been a momentary qualm that had passed through his mind as he sorted through his library that afternoon, and thought about his life and legacy. He was grateful he could express his innermost thoughts, even the deeply vulnerable ones, with Vanessa, without fear of shame or misunderstanding. He realized now that this is one of the many things he had missed all the years he had spent as a widower after his first wife, dear Beth, had died so young. Especially as the pastor of a church, Rex found himself at the giving end of counseling, and sometimes he yearned to have more avenues to share his own uncertainties and dark moments, his own occasional insecurities.

He remembered fondly the day he and Vanessa had met. Or, more accurately, met again. Their first meeting was long ago when Rex was a young minister in Chicago. It was the late 1960s. He had been deeply involved in community activism, marching in civil rights causes and anti-war marches and just generally doing what he felt was right for his church and his country, what his conscience and his faith told him to do. It was a rough and tumble time, and life moved too dynamically to chronicle. Rex spent most of the first half of his ministerial years in this kind of work, living and being a pastor in urban areas where crisis and poverty were equally matched by warm feats of human spirit. It was petty politics that eventually chased him out of this setting, inner squabbling among church leaders, and, in the end, the toll on his family was too great; Rex left the city with deep grief and moved on to a more suburban church outside Chicago, where he found people to be much the same, the good and the bad, the weak and the strong, even when the outward appearances and inward assumptions were significantly different. The new environment did not make Rex happier.

But long before that move, Rex was an idealistic dreamer and warrior. And self-inspired by his own hope for radical transformation within the church and society, believing that elevating people out of the cycle of poverty and inequality was the most important mission of his faith, his sincerity and fervor consequently provided inspiration for others. He preached one day at a church gathering in Chicago, where many of the urban churches had come together to promote community service, political activism, as well as spiritual renewal. A college student was in attendance that day, home from school for the summer. She had come to the rally with her mother and sisters. There was something about the young Rex Randall that captivated her, even though on the surface he was so different from her, or perhaps because he was. Or maybe the only difference was that she was black and he was white. Regardless of the reason, the sincerity and fervor of the man impressed her for a lifetime, and when a young man from her church later grumbled, "That white boy can't speak for us," she flared to Rex's defense and for anyone working together to fight for justice for all. This did not earn her favor with the distrusting young man, but that day at the rally is when Vanessa embarked on her own path of church and community activism. Perhaps this commitment would have happened for Vanessa anyway, but it was flavored with the inspiration of Rex Randall's bold words that day in Chicago.

Rex had no idea. As the messenger, he often struggled, even doubted, but clearly the message had touched at least one person.

Over the many years that passed since that day, both Rex and Vanessa led parallel lives of adventures and misadventures and daily work. Vanessa married, left Chicago with her new husband and moved to Boston where their three children were born. Soon after sinking new roots in Boston, she divorced, but decided not to leave her new home. She found employment as an editor, but, besides raising her children, she found her passion within her church and neighborhood.

In Chicago, meanwhile, Rex and Beth had a son and a daughter. It was a good marriage, cut short by Beth's death. After her death, the kids grown, Rex, now working in the suburbs, tired of that life, and moved east to Pine Junction, Massachusetts. This move more than satisfied his need to be surrounded by trees in a small town where he could focus upon the people of the parish, as well as the more contemplative aspects of his faith and life itself. His life as a fiery orator seemed in the far past, yet despite his new peaceful demeanor, he remained a strong out-of-the-box thinker. That would never change, no matter how he had learned to honor traditions.

Decades passed since that long-ago rally in Chicago. And then one afternoon, while on an excursion to Boston soon after he finally retired, Rex was walking out of a coffee shop, nose deep in a book, and he bumped smack into Vanessa Jefferson, who was herself looking the other way while talking on her phone. Fortunately Rex's coffee had long gone cold and it did not burn her when it spilled all over the front of the dress she had purchased especially for her meeting with a new client.

The rest is history. Rex's apologies, awkward scrambles to get her napkins, a realization that he couldn't and shouldn't dab off the coffee stains himself, and yet an electrifying knowledge that he would have loved to run his hands over her lovely breasts under the deep green fabric of the dress. In her annoyance, the normally forgiving Vanessa told Rex what she thought of his carelessness and told him to watch where he was going next time and just in general chewed him out, but he only looked at her in wonderment and gave her a chagrined smile. She softened, and then, despite the decades of transformed appearance, slowly a recognition came to her, and she burst out, "Rex Randall?"

He stared at her, baffled.

Vanessa did have her interview with the client in the coffee shop after washing out the worst of the coffee stains herself, but first she managed to hand Rex her business card and practically ordered him to call her.

Their romance couldn't have surprised them more. And it led to a lovely wedding and ten days in the sunshine of Jamaica where Vanessa and Rex enjoyed the warmth of her cousin's hospitality even while they worried over the poverty of the beautiful island.

Now tonight was their three-hundred-sixty-fifth day celebration and reassessment date.

Over dinner they took stock.

"You go first, Vanessa. After all, you made the biggest change when you married me. I'm in the same house and in the same little town, but you made a major move. What are your feelings now? Stay? Go? Where? When? Yes? No? How's it been?"

Vanessa threw back her head and laughed from her heart." Much to my complete and total surprise, I'm happy as a clam right here in Pine Junction. I knew I would be happy with you, Rex, but I never dreamed I could be so content in this teeny town, with the same folks to see day after day. I have shocked my friends and my kids. Lord, they just can't believe it."

"Yes, I remember the comment Roshawna made at the wedding. Something like, 'Momma will be happy in a little town when pigs fly!' "

"Well, Rex darling, those pigs are flying higher than the clouds right now!"

"You really mean that? I've sensed that you were happy here, but I have to tell you that I never thought you'd be able to adapt so well. I really figured we would be heading back to the city to live out the rest of our lives and I was, and am, quite happy to do that. But you really like it here? You've found enough to do?"

"Happy as can be, Reverend Rex. I guess I was ready for a change, and ready for my life to slow down, although there is a project just waiting for me outside Amherst with those farm worker children and mothers who don't have health care." She brought herself back to the topic at hand. "I think our time in Jamaica might be part of it. I looked around at how that part of my family lives, how simple and easy it is . . . I don't mean easy money-wise, but just at how they live in a small community at a slow pace, and I started thinking, 'This is my heritage too.' I was born there and spent my first five years with my grandparents before my mother fetched me to the city. Then, of course, after that I was raised in the hub of Chicago where there was action hopping all the time, but maybe that isn't completely who I am. Maybe I've got some of that small town girl deep inside me, too. Maybe Pine Junction is helping me find that. Or maybe I'm so happy to be with you that I can't see straight yet. You figure it out, I'm just enjoying myself."

She gave a big laugh and added a teaser, although it contained a reasonable note. "I'll happily sign up for another three-hundred-sixty-five days, and then we can talk again."

Rex squeezed her hand over the table, but cleared his throat tentatively.

"Well, given that, I don't know how to say this to you, but my sweet, I'm getting restless here in Pine Junction recently. Oh, I've loved this place and my role here. But, my role is over now. The new pastor has been called. I've taken a huge step away from my work, my calling. I still have my dear friends here, but lately I have been finding myself dreaming of something new, that I need to be someplace else."

He looked at her and Vanessa nodded for him to continue. "This may sound dramatic, but I've been feeling the call of the sea."

Vanessa laughed, "So, Jamaica got to you too?"

"Maybe, hadn't thought about that. But the sea that calls me is not the Caribbean, not even the Atlantic. I'm thinking of the Pacific. Maybe it's a call to go home. I was born out in the West, and lately I've been thinking of the pounding waves on the rocky shores, so wild, so dangerous, so open. So very beautiful. Kind of a far cry from the warm waters of the islands, I'm afraid." He suddenly felt apologetic as he looked at his wife. How could he hope she would feel the same draw he had been experiencing? The wild Pacific coastline was vastly different from the East Coast shore she knew in Boston, and even more opposite from the waters of her Jamaican roots.

But Vanessa was open to hear. "Tell me more, Rex. Remind me about your childhood."

"I've told you that my dad and his dad and all my uncles were, every one of them, loggers in far Northern California."

Vanessa interrupted him with a laugh. "I still find that ironic, Rex. You, the consummate tree-hugger, and you came from a family of loggers! Sorry, go on."

Rex's smile was wry. "Yes, true, but I think you'll see how this all came about. One day Dad came home from work. I remember it clearly. I was about seven years old. He walked in the house, put down his lunch box and told my mom, 'Celeste, I just felled my last tree.' My mom just stood there and looked at him, wondering if he was out of his mind. You see, her family were all loggers, too. It was all they knew. So, what was my dad saying? But he was serious. He told me the story when I was older, that his crew had been working on a particularly large tree that day, I figure now it was old growth, and when it finally fell, something happened to him. I guess it was like a spiritual experience for him, from out of nowhere, or maybe it had been building up inside of him. I don't know. You and I know what spiritual experiences are like, Vanessa. Sometimes they just come out of nowhere and hit you on the head, but usually when you look back at it later, you can see how everything was surging towards that moment."

Rex took his last sip of wine.

"So, true to his word, Dad left the next day on the bus out of the logging town and on up to Portland where he walked the streets for two days looking for work. No internet searches in those days. He was walking by a big bookstore and he laughed to himself. 'Maybe some of the trees I cut were made into these books,' is what he was thinking as he looked at the store window and noticed a help wanted sign. So he walked in. They were looking for someone strong to do lifting and shelving and storage and moving of books. Dad met their requirements. They gave him a two-week trial period.

"Dad called my mom and said, 'Pack our stuff, settle up at the company store, get Donna and Rex's school records, and put some gas in the truck. I will be home in two weeks. We're moving to Portland.' "

Rex laughed. "It wasn't that easy for my mom, I can tell you that. I'm kind of skipping over all of that transition. In those days wives generally had no choice but to go along with their husband's plans, but my mom must have been very flexible or ready for an adventure herself, because she adjusted quite well in a short time. But, long story short, we moved to Portland and I fell in love with books at the bookstore where my dad worked for the rest of his life. He never regretted his move and gradually the extended family came around to accept my father's defection, at least enough to be on speaking terms. Donna and I joined a Methodist church with my mom. Although my dad didn't join the church, he taught me to respect the spirit within nature. My mom, much to everyone's surprise, became very interested in social justice work at a time when no one really knew to call it that. I guess you can see where I picked up my inclinations!"

Vanessa smiled while she entertained the memory of her first encounter with the handsome young minister, with his long reddish hair and his contagious passion for justice.

Rex got up to start clearing the table. But Vanessa told him to sit down.

"Okay, so you came to seminary in the east and then ministered in Chicago where you inspired this college student - oh, let's be honest, where I first fell in love with you. Then you had the all-white suburban church, and then Pine Junction. But, tell me more about this call to the sea. Or, is it a call to go home?"

"This is not very clearly thought out yet, Vanessa, and of course all my ideas only go as far as where you and I want to go together. I just appreciate being able to explore these dreams with you freely."

Rex pulled up his chair with a glint in his eyes that made him look like a school boy. Fifty years fell away as he told Vanessa about his experiences as a child with his dad: going tide pooling, body surfing the cold waves on summer trips, the coastal Oregon summer vacations, driving up and down the coastline on the precarious highway, seeing the dark sea stacks just offshore that so distinctly marked the Oregon coast. He talked of taking the ferry off the Washington coast with his parents and sister. He regaled her with his excitement at seeing orcas and dolphins arching through the waves, and of going salmon fishing with his father. He spoke of the rain forest and the trees; always, always the trees. When he mentioned going down to northern California to walk through the giant redwoods, his eyes grew misty with wonder all over again.

His stories pricked Vanessa's memory and she interrupted, "Mendocino! That's what you're making me remember - my first honeymoon, of all things!" And she laughed at the thought.

Rex came back out of his own reminiscing to listen.

"Rex, when I was first married to my husband, Jermaine, all those centuries ago, he took me to Mendocino for our honeymoon. Let me tell you, no one else in my family from the South Side of Chicago went to California for honeymoons, or if they did, they went to Hollywood or Palm Springs or someplace like that. But Jermaine always wanted to try something new, and he'd heard about Mendocino from a client and was set that we should go out there. Jermaine and I were real happy together for our first few years, and we sure had fun on our honeymoon!" She gave a laugh that turned into a sigh, ". . . before the reality of daily living and three kids interfered with his fun times . . ."

Dismissing this long-forgiven history, she smiled at Rex. "I remember the Pacific being big and powerful, just spectacular. Awesome would be the word. Magical. We had a rental car and we drove up and down on that steep highway. Took my breath away, 'cause I thought we might be going to sail off the road and down a million feet to the rocks and ocean. But, I loved it. I loved it. I felt so alive."

Rex and Vanessa looked at each other. Would they do it? It was enough for tonight to know that each was more than satisfied to be together wherever that might be. And if the spirit moved them in one direction or another, they would be prepared to follow.

For the rest of the evening, feeling like one foot was still happily planted in Pine Junction and one foot was edging towards the door, the two sat down to watch their favorite television drama together, relaxed in the make-believe lives of the BBC.

But, Rex considered what Vanessa's children would say if their independent mother, their anchor, would move three thousand miles away from Boston; Pine Junction had been an adjustment for them as it was.

And in turn, Vanessa wondered how Rex would feel to leave his friends in Pine Junction.

When he was sinking into sleep that night, listening to Vanessa's breathing next to him, Rex himself reflected on this same thought. He had loved his time as pastor in Pine Junction. All the ritual and ordinary functions of church life had centered him, while the exasperating times, dealing with the sometimes irritating idiosyncrasies of individual church members, he took lovingly in stride. And then there were the sublime moments, which for Rex often meant musical experiences, and also included times of transformation among his members as he walked by their sides through births and weddings, and sickness and death.

He reflected that his life in Pine Junction was greatly colored by his experience with the Sanchez family. It had been eight years now since the explosive events of 2005, when Mateo Schumacher, grandson of his faithful parishioners, Pedro and Victoria Sanchez, had returned to Pine Junction at Rex's own calling. (That call had been prompted by his concern for the mental health of Mateo's mother, Cecilia.) The events that had unfolded at that point still astounded Rex to this day: Victoria's unexpected death, Pedro's son Javier's sudden appearance, the assault on Mateo by Javier's son, and Mateo's resulting coma. And, with all of that, what would at one time have been the most traumatic revelation of all, had been placed into perspective with amazing quickness - when Cecilia finally told Mateo the identity of his birth father. Retelling it now in his mind, all these events sounded like a soap opera; but, as Rex bore witness, these experiences were all very real. Reality, he reflected, sometimes played out in unbelievable fashion.

Secret after secret unraveled within the Sanchez family and it had been dramatic. All in all, though, the outcome was positive. Now in 2013, the family members were more connected than ever.

Before Pedro became too disabled to travel, he had taken his grandson Mateo to Arizona with him as a companion where he revisited his long-repressed past life. How much of this past he revealed to Mateo, Rex was not entirely sure, but it seemed to have been a therapeutic trip for everyone. Mateo's brother Rowan had not gone along because he had entered nursing school; but, along with Mateo, Pedro had invited his newly discovered son, Javier. In the company of Javier and Mateo, Pedro had re-entered the Arizona town he left behind many decades before. Rex heard they had visited the grave of Pedro's sister, Maria. And he knew they had located some of the family members of his former neighbors, giving Pedro a chance to repay in person his deep gratitude to the Gonzalez descendents for all their family had done for him, for giving a poor boy love, and a new vision of how to live.

Although Javier and Mateo came to share strong respect for each other, Mateo had only a wary cordiality with

Javier's son, Armando, and the two cousins spent little time together in the eight years since their altercation. Armando had served a short prison term for the assault, and was now living near his father in New Mexico, by starts and stops, rebuilding his life. Mateo, having to take time to rebuild his brain health after the coma, had wisely not wasted energy with ill will. Nonetheless, Mateo had shared with Rex that he still occasionally recalled the rush of unwanted emotions that he experienced when he first met Armando all those years ago. It was, he said, humbling and instructive.

Rex thought of Mateo often. After his recovery, he had gone to college at last. Some expected that he would enter the teaching field, given the family history, but he discovered he had a head for business along with his love of music. Mateo was currently manager to several bands, handling their business and financial matters. Included among his clients was his biological father, Dane Faber, now in his sixties, whose singing career was going strong, having a husky and appealing voice that was timeless. And even more surprising, Mateo's other father, Warren Schumacher, sometimes helped Mateo as a legal advisor for his new business. Sometimes Rex just had to chuckle at how life unfolded!

Mateo and Catherine, his cello-playing girlfriend, had married. She found a steady home with the string quartet, Tapestry, traveling around the world from their home in Brooklyn. The last time Mateo had been in Pine Junction to visit, he told Rex that he and Catherine felt it was now or never if they were going to have children, so it looked like things might change dramatically for the young couple soon.

Rex looked at the clock on the nightstand: 2:00 in the morning. Retirement meant that nothing demanded an early rising. He yawned luxuriously, moved to his side to spoon up against Vanessa, and felt near sleep, but before rest came to him, he recalled one of the most moving experiences of his time in Pine Junction.

That experience came when Pedro Sanchez passed away, just over three years ago, in 2009. As Pedro lay near death, the whole family had gathered. There was an aura of peacefulness. Their father's illness and transition had been prolonged and his daughters were glad to be there to see him to the other side. Maria, Cecilia, and Olivia thought of their mother many times during Pedro's last weeks. When Victoria had suddenly died in 2005, all three daughters felt they had been kicked in the center of their being. They no longer blamed Victoria for that kick. They had found affection and even more respect in their memories of their mother. But the experience of her death still evoked pain, for there had been no time for reconciliation or tenderness or goodbyes.

But now they circled around Pedro's bed, with Cecilia holding one of his hands and Maria the other. Pedro could no longer talk to them, but they felt sure he could hear them. As his grandfather's breathing became shallow and uneven, Mateo played his guitar on through the hours, every song he could think of that his grandfather loved, from the Mexican music of his childhood to the blues of the City, to the classical music of the church and symphony.

Rex had been honored to be present with Pedro's family that night. Now, almost four years later as he finally moved towards sleep, Rex could picture each one in that room with Pedro. Vic was steadfast by Cecilia's side. Pedro's other grandchildren, Rowan and Julia, were there. Catherine had come too, her new wedding band flashing in the soft light as she placed her hand on Mateo's shoulder. Maria and her wife, Rosemary, Olivia and Brad, all were there, together, united, helping Pedro Sanchez complete his odyssey. When Javier had arrived from New Mexico, only an hour before Pedro finally slipped away, the family made room for him without any hesitation. Rex, from his position as an observer, could see the emotion in this man who had so recently found his family under such turbulent circumstances. Maria moved aside and motioned for Javier to come and sit in her chair. He paused, unsure, but she insisted, and so he came to hold his father's hand in that last hour. Rex could see that the secrets had been revealed and no longer held the power to limit and hurt these fine people.

As an hour passed in suspended time on Pedro's dying day, Rex felt a shift. He said to Mateo, "'Simple Gifts.' Your grandfather loves that song." This family choir of complex and imperfect angels sang Pedro on his journey, a journey begun in sorrow, but now bonded by love. Somewhere from not so far away, Señora Gonzalez whispered into

Pedro's ear . . . "Don't worry, mijo, come on home." Pedro heard it.

Yes, Rex had thought on that night, and now again, a lifetime of sermons couldn't match the impact of that night.

But finally Rex's mind let the Sanchez family rest in peace, and he cuddled near his Vanessa's warm body to slip into a deep and peaceful sleep, dreaming only of his future with her.

The End

ACKNOWLEDGEMENTS

I would first like to acknowledge my (fictional) characters from Pine Junction. The folks from *Junctions* took a powerful hold of me and would not let go until they had whispered missing pieces of their stories, a background of experiences that molded who they were. Over the last few years since *Junctions* was completed, they constantly visited me - while trying to sleep, in the middle of a concert at Davies Hall, on a BART train - and each new piece of story I heard, accumulated to explain why they behaved the way they did in the pages of *Junctions*. Think me crazy if you will, but I swear to you that these characters have a life of their own, and I am merely the conduit for their stories. Thus, *Journeys* was born and brought forth.

I also should make mention of a two of my many writing heroes whose books have specifically influenced *Journeys*. I have long enjoyed the writings of Wendell Berry, both for his settings and storytelling, and also for his overlapping stories, where the characters we have already come to love, reappear in another story as background figures, or at a different time in their life. When I first read *Olive Kittredge* by Elizabeth Strout, I was captivated by the structure of the book, where the cranky and yet painfully endearing Olive was woven in and out of the stories in various ways. In like manner, it is my hope that the stories within *Journeys* will enhance the anchor novel, *Junctions*, by moving many different characters on and off center stage

My thanks to my beta readers, Jinx McCombs, Paul Nordstrand, Judy Vargas and Karen Mireau - their feedback all along the way was vital. And a very special thanks to my own dear David, for our countless breakfast reading sessions during which he proved that a finance wizard can also be a creative writing advisor.

Cousin Jinx provided the wonderful poem that begins *Journeys*. I loved this poem from the first time I read it, and it belongs in *Journeys* in a profound way. Once again thanks to Cynthia Leslie-Bole for her enthusiasm that goes above and beyond her role as my professional editor. Dario Sanchez-Kennedy designed another stunning cover. Having provided his skill for proof copy-editing with *Junctions*, friend III came back for more, much to my gratitude. I send thanks to those who approached me after reading *Junctions* and said to me, "I hope you have a story in your next book about _____." Your queries made me wonder myself, and, before you know it, there came another story. Derrick's story is directly due to Cindy Conejo's question, and Dane's story came out of Shari Nagi's wish to know more about him.

My love to sons Alex and Jackson. Our many conversations about writing and every other topic imaginable, happily knit together the threads of my mothering life and my writing life.

There is no question that life in our United States and across the world is especially challenging now in 2017. I want to believe in a compassionate and creative future for my children and grandchildren - and for all children everywhere on this earth - but I must be willing to speak up and work for such a world. With my novels, I want to share my conviction that how we treat each other does matter - within families, within our government, and within our global community.

C'Anna Bergman-Hill

FURTHERMORE

There is one character noticeably missing from *Journeys,* and that is Maria Sanchez, Pedro's oldest daughter. Maria began to intrigue me along the way, and soon she had more than a short story to tell; she had a full length novel. In *Pathways,* the final book of the *Junctions* series, not only is Maria's life revealed, but we get a glimpse of the childhood days of all three Sanchez daughters.

Despite her successful career, Maria perpetually experiences a complicated relationship life, but just when she determines to live a life free of romance, she finds out what love can be. Also central to Maria's life is her struggle with her mother, Victoria. In the pages of *Pathways,* the reader has an opportunity to get to know Victoria better, and will feel frustration and sympathy, both. And finally, in *Pathways,* Maria and the rest of the family learn the details of Pedro's World War II experiences and more about that terrible time in world history. It is to these World War II veterans, all veterans, and most importantly, to those who work for peace, that *Pathways* is dedicated.

You'll meet some new friends in *Pathways* and renew acquaintance with old Pine Junction friends. Coming soon, *Pathways*.